# ABOARD THE WISHING STAR

## DEBRA PARMLEY

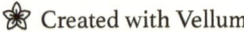

*To my husband, Mike.*
*I'm glad they brought you back. Thank you for the lesson*
*that life can be short and none of us are promised*
*tomorrow. This moment is all we have.*

# CHAPTER ONE

"Oh my God, they lost my luggage."

Kara, wide eyed with worry, turned to look at her best friend Viv. The luggage carousel had stopped moving and the other passengers from their flight were long gone. "What am I gonna do? I can't go on a seven day Caribbean cruise with only this."

She lifted her carry on, which contained a swimsuit, a pair of shorts and a tee shirt to change into once she reached Florida, and the winter coat she'd stuffed inside that she wouldn't need until she returned to Ohio.

The only other people in the room were passengers from another flight who'd gathered around a different luggage carousel to wait for their bags.

Kara's phone rang.

*Daryl.*

"Hello."

"I thought you were going to call me when you landed."

"I'm kind of busy right now, Daryl. Gotta go. My luggage is missing."

"What?"

"Bye, Daryl. I can't talk now." Kara hung up. The phone rang again. She glanced at it and turned it off. He never seemed to take the hint when she said she was busy. It was just easier to turn the phone off.

"Girl, you need a break from your boss. Doesn't that man understand you're on vacation?"

"He just wanted to know I got here okay. Viv, what am I gonna do? I can't sail without my luggage."

"Hang on." Viv approached the opening where the luggage emerged and leaned across the stopped conveyer belt to shout into the dark hole. "Hey, anyone back there?"

Kara's mouth dropped open.

*My God, I can't believe she's doing that.*

A man shouted back, "What do you think you're doing? You can't come back here."

Kara gasped.

*Oh my God. They'll arrest her. They'll think she's a terrorist.*

"I'm not trying to come back there. But my friend's luggage hasn't come out yet," Viv yelled back. "And I wondered if you'd all gone home."

The man laughed. "What's the flight number?"

Vivian glanced over at the monitor that showed the flight arrival from Columbus, Ohio. "Five seventy one."

"We've sent everything out from that flight."

"This is unbelievable," Kara said. "What am I gonna do?"

"They'll find it. You need to go report it so we can get going."

"Is there anything I can do to help?"

Kara turned and looked up into deep brown eyes that smiled down on her with concern. She caught her breath. He was at least six-foot to her five-foot-seven and had broad shoulders and a deep tan.

"My friend's luggage is missing and we're leaving on a cruise within hours. That's why she's upset. But thank you for offering. Viviane Tate." Viv stuck out her hand and Mr. Tall-Dark-and-Handsome shook it.

"Nate Cooper." He turned to Kara and held out his hand.

"Kara Worth." She put her hand in his and felt the warm strength of his fingers enclose it, making her skin tingle.

"That's a beautiful name, Kara." He smiled, which warmed her to her toes.

"Thank you."

"Pleased to meet you both." His smile lit up the

room and the rumble of his voice took her breath away. It was the kind of voice she could've closed her eyes and listened to all day.

"Likewise," Viv said. "Where are you headed?"

He let go of Kara's hand to turn to Viv again, and Kara felt the loss of its warmth.

"I'm sailing on The Wishing Star."

"So are we!" Viv moved closer to him. "Are you traveling alone?"

"With my cousin."

"Kara hasn't had a vacation in years. She's a widow." Viv shook her head. "Terrible thing. He was shot at a gas station right in front of her."

*Great. Does she have to bring that up to everyone we meet?*

Nate glanced at Kara concern in his eyes. "You're much too young to be a widow. That must have been hard."

"Yes, can you imagine?" Viv grasped his arm and led him away, lowering her voice.

Kara's jaw dropped. *I cannot believe this. What is she doing? She has a boyfriend.*

"I'm going over to report my luggage missing," she called over to Viv.

Viv nodded at her and kept talking to Nate.

Kara found the counter where she had to fill out a form and the attendant assured her they'd find her bags and send them on.

"You can't send them to me. I'll be out in the middle of the ocean. I'm going on a cruise. This is a nightmare."

"Calm down, Kara," Viv said from behind Kara as she approached.

"That's easy for you to say. Your luggage hasn't gone missing." She glanced behind Viv and saw Nate heading out the revolving door. She wondered what Viv had said to him.

"You can borrow a few of my things. Don't let this ruin your trip."

"Thanks, Viv."

"I'm sorry about your luggage, miss," the attendant said. "If we don't find it before you sail, we will send it to your first port of call."

"But we won't be in port until Tuesday," Kara said.

"We'll do the best we can."

Viv placed her hand on Kara's arm. "There's nothing more you can do. Come on. Maybe the bags will be on the ship waiting for you."

"I hope so."

They boarded the bus, which would take them to the pier, and Viv chattered about nightclubs and bars on the ship while Kara tried to keep her mind on the conversation and not on her missing luggage or whether she'd see Nate again. After all it had been a year since she'd seen Viv. She was looking forward to their time together. Viv was her oldest and dearest friend, and they'd be celebrating New Years together this year on a cruise ship.

Port Canaveral was full of ships, and as their bus drew nearer, Kara and Viv watched through the window looking for their ship. Their ship was the tallest of them all and even larger than Kara had imagined.

"Wow. It has to be at least two hundred feet tall," Kara said. Two large red and black smoke stacks stood atop the white ship, which had *The Wishing Star* painted on the side.

"Wow is right. See. You won't even know you're on the ocean. We'll be so busy you won't have time to be scared."

"The website photos didn't do it justice." Kara had haunted the Internet in the days leading up to the trip. "No wonder Daryl said they're like a floating city." She turned to look at Viv. "I won't be scared. I took that beginner's swim class, remember?"

"Oh yeah. That's right. Have you made your wish yet?"

"No," Kara said.

"Promise me you'll make one before we set sail."

"All right, I'll think of something."

*But I don't know what to wish for. And wishes don't always come true.* Wishes didn't bring Neil back. Kara knew nothing could. Not even prayer. *Sometimes the things you want most you can't have.* It was better not to want anything so much.

It had been so long since she'd wished for anything. She stared out the window at the towering ship as they drew closer.

*Wishes are for little girls who still believe in fairy tales and Santa Clause. Not for grown women who know how life really is.*

"Are you thinking of your wish?" Viv nudged her elbow. "What is it?"

"I'm not going to think of one with you elbowing me."

Viv isn't gonna let this go.

Kara sighed. *I better come up with one. I have to wish for something because I promised. But it needs to be something small. Something that won't hurt or disappoint when it doesn't come true.*

They got off the bus, collected their carry-ons, and entered the cruise terminal with their tickets out, ready to board.

Kara turned her phone back on while they waited in line to get their photos taken for the room key/I.D. card they'd use to board. She'd intended to call Daryl back until she saw she had six calls from him. On the last call he'd left a message.

"Damn it, Kara, turn on your phone and call me back."

Frowning, she deleted it. He could wait. It was their turn for photos.

"Smile Kara," Viv said. "Girl, if anyone needs a vacation it's you."

Kara forced a smile she didn't quite feel with her mind still on Daryl.

"This is going to be awesome," Viv said, her movements getting even bouncier as they boarded the ship.

Kara's smile returned for real this time.

The ship's interior welcomed them with a refined grace and overflowing elegance. Kara breathed in the scent of lemon polish and fresh flowers. Brass surfaces gleamed and bright murals colored the walls. The elevator made no sound other than a soft female voice saying, "doors opening now" or "doors closing now."

Kara tried to allow the gracefulness of the ship to seep over her to forget she was on the ocean and had a fear of deep water. If she hadn't won this vacation for two, she'd never have paid to go on a cruise. But Viv was excited enough for both of them and her enthusiasm was always contagious. It had been a long time since she and Viv did anything fun together.

What could be better than a trip with her best friend?

"I'm ready to be pampered," she said to let Viv know she was trying.

"Me too."

On the door to their cabin a label with gold

letters read Mrs. Kara Worth and Ms. Vivian Tate. The small room designed in peach tones comforted like an elegant cave. On the desk a card of heavy white stock announced the cabin steward's name and extension. Fresh fruit and bottled water stood beside it.

A knock sounded on the door and Vivian opened it.

"Good evening. I am Bertrand, your cabin steward. If there is anything you need ...?"

"Nothing at the moment," Viv said.

"Your life jackets are in the closet, and your muster station, where you'll go for the life boat drill, is on the Promenade deck. When the bell rings for the lifeboat drill the crew will direct you."

"Righto. We'll be ready."

He moved on to the next cabin and knocked at the door.

Inside the cabin, Viv opened the wall safe and put her wallet and jewelry inside. "I'm putting my watch in here," she said removing it. "We don't have to be anywhere on time this week, except dinner."

"Good idea." Kara took off her watch and handed it over along with her wallet and jewelry, setting them inside as well.

Her phone went off again and her face fell when she saw it was Daryl.

Viv grabbed it out of her hand. "If you don't tell that son of a bitch to stop calling you, I will."

"I can't tell my boss that."

Viv turned the phone off and locked it in the safe. "Well, you're not at work now. You're officially on vacation. Soon to be at sea, where cell phone reception is sometimes spotty. Whatever he wants, it can wait."

"Viv, I really should see what he wants. I can't keep avoiding him. What if it's something important?"

A bell sounded three short rings. "This is the captain. All passengers and crew report to their muster stations."

"I don't have time to call him back now," Kara said, as she looked in one side of the closet. "Where are the life jackets?"

Viv found the jackets in the other closet and handed one to Kara. "Atta girl. Plenty of time to deal with your boss later. Like when this cruise is over. Come on, let's go."

The crew directed them to their muster stations.

Kara stood in the evening sun eyeing the lifeboats. "They're such small boats for such a big ocean. I hope we never have to step into one because the ship is sinking."

*Oh God. What will I do if the ship starts to sink?*

"Kara there will never be another Titanic. Ships today don't sink," Viv said.

"That's not true. Don't you remember that Italian cruise ship that struck a reef in the Mediterranean and all those people had to jump into the water?" Kara shivered.

"Stop it, Kara. This ship is not going to sink."

Kara bit her lip.

The officer in charge of their station paced with a clipboard, waiting for the last of the passengers. He tapped it with his pen, which for some reason made her more nervous.

*Why didn't the passengers hurry? Hadn't they heard the captain? The ship couldn't sail until the crew accounted for all the passengers. An emergency would be just like this. They wouldn't lower the boats until everyone was here and counted. Passengers should take this more seriously.*

The close crowd and the perfume of the woman beside her were overpowering as the evening sun beat down. Kara closed her eyes, hoping she wouldn't end up with a headache.

Viv had turned to the redheaded woman beside her to chat about Italian men, especially the officers onboard.

"I just love Italian men. And you say all the officers on this ship are Italian?" Viv's eyes lit up. "Isn't that unusual on an American ship?"

"This isn't the military, dearie. The crew is multinational." The redhead laughed.

"Hey, Viv," Kara said.

But Viv either hadn't heard her or was ignoring her.

Kara fumbled with the orange life jacket. Her hands shook.

*What if this was a real emergency?*

She'd only just learned to swim two years ago in the timid non-swimmers class at the gym. Six months before Neil was killed, and she hadn't swum since.

*No, don't think about the ship going down. Don't think about trying to swim in the ocean with a defective life jacket.*

But the thoughts came anyway.

"Stupid life jacket," she muttered under her breath as she struggled with it. More passengers crowding into their area made everyone shift sideways.

A voice behind her said, "Here sweetheart, let me help."

*Oh, that voice.*

The back of her neck tingled.

Embarrassment flooded over her, making it harder to fasten the jacket.

Nate stepped in front of her, deep brown eyes looking down at her as he smiled and reached both arms around behind her back. "Hello again," he said and smiled deeper, his eyes gazing into hers. "We have to stop meeting like this." Then he winked.

His face was bronzed by wind and sun, and he projected a magnetic self-confidence along with a generous smile.

"Hello," she murmured, blushing as his scent, spicy and male, and his nearness made her senses spin. She felt dizzy. Between the heat of his body and the heat of the sun she grew warmer and more flushed.

"Your straps are twisted."

She watched his lips as he spoke and her pulse raced.

"Let me fix them for you."

He towered over her. She had to look up to look into his eyes. Brown eyes that sparkled as he untwisted the straps.

She nodded. The blush spread across her face.

His hand brushed the small of her back as he untwisted the straps, sending a tingle up her spine. He was so close, yet the bulky lifejacket held her head up and covered her chest.

Yet it wasn't only the man's sexiness and the sudden attraction that nearly did her in but the tender way he administered to her. The way she felt cared for. Something she hadn't felt for a long time.

Her body came alive as if one touch had turned on the floodlights. And the part deep within her that wanted to be cared for and loved made her ache with need.

Pulling the straps together in front, he snapped the vest tight. "There, that's better."

She didn't look up into his eyes. Instead her eyes

traced the stubble on his chin. *Who would have thought a man's stubbly chin could be so sexy?*

She wanted to reach up and touch it.

Knowing she should thank him, instead she stood, frozen, bared to her soul. If she said one word she feared all the pent up loneliness inside her would come pouring out.

Now all the passengers were accounted for, and the captain's voice came over the loudspeaker, interrupting what either of them might have said.

Nate stood for one more brief moment looking down into her eyes, his teeth white against his tan, his intent brown eyes upon hers, before he winked again and stepped back behind her.

Kara was intensely aware of his presence though she tried to ignore it, to focus on the captain's instructions. It was important to pay attention. This information could save her life if the ship started to sink.

She glanced down at the small whistle and plastic light hanging from her vest like children's toys.

*The light would act as a beacon. But how could anyone see that tiny thing in the vast ocean?*

*Don't think about the ship going down like the Titanic. Don't.*

The evening sun beat down, and she longed to retreat to their cool cabin. Viv moved over next to her. "When the drill is over let's put on our swimsuits and try out the hot tub."

"That and a frosty pina colada sounds good."

Kara wondered if Nate had overheard and if he'd look for her later. She wasn't going to say anything to Viv after the way Viv flirted with him in the airport, but secretly Kara made one small wish. Viv had been after her to make one and they were, after all, sailing on the *Wishing Star*.

# CHAPTER TWO

"*H*ow do I look?" Viv spun in a gold bikini.

"Stunning as always," Kara said.

"Stop tugging at your cleavage," Viv said. "You look great. Guys will come flocking. Just wait and see."

Kara looked in the mirror. "I'm too pale."

"Not for long." Viv pulled on a black mesh cover-up Kara could see her swimsuit through. "Come on, hurry. We don't want to miss the bon voyage party."

Kara tied the red and gold sarong she'd borrowed from Viv around her waist. They headed to the top deck to check the view and then went down to the deck below, where two hot tubs stood on each side of the pool. The pool had a bar at one end and a grill at the other. Waiters in Hawaiian shirts handed out umbrella drinks while a Calypso band played. Kara and Vivian reached the hot tub and Kara dropped her things on a chair and eased down into the warm, bubbling water, wiggling her toes while Viv went up to the bar to get two pina coladas.

Calypso music played as the ship eased out of the dock heading for open seas. She could see another ship in the distance, and a third a bit farther out, one following the other like ducks in a row. She was so busy watching, lost in thought she didn't notice Nate until he spoke.

"Alone at last." Nate's voice was resonant and sensual, and his words wrapped around Kara as she turned to look at him. He winked at her, climbed into the hot tub, and then sat, leaning his powerful, well-muscled body back against the hot tub. "Did they find your luggage yet?"

She tried not to stare at Nate's bare chest. "No."

"It could be down below clearing customs even as we speak."

"I hope so."

He glanced at her swimsuit.

The swimsuit that fit her all too snug.

"At least you have a swimsuit. What else do you need on a cruise?" He winked.

"Well perhaps a nice dress to wear to dinner."

"I'm sure your luggage will turn up soon."

"I hope so."

"So, we're sailing on the *Wishing Star*. Have you made a wish yet?"

*Was he psychic?*

She wouldn't admit she'd wished to see him again tonight.

"I made a wish. But I can't tell you what my wish is."

"Because you're afraid it might not come true?"

"No." She smiled.

"I'll tell you mine later if it comes true."

"I hope you get your wish."

"And I hope you get every one of yours."

*He couldn't know she was full of unfulfilled wishes.*

If she were honest with herself, she'd been making wishes for the past month. Whispered wishes in the dark.

"I hope so too."

Viv came back with two pina coladas, took one look at Nate, and practically purred. "Well, hello again."

"Hello," he responded with a polite smile as she handed Kara a drink. He returned his full attention to Kara, his gaze interested and warm "Kara and I were just talking about wishes."

"Well, tell her to hurry up and make one or she's gonna miss out. She doesn't listen to me."

"I suspect she's already made her wish." He smiled.

Kara returned his smile. It was nice having him take up for her.

A man who resembled Nate entered the hot tub.

"This is my cousin, Adam. Adam, this is Kara," Nate draped his arm across the top of the hot tub behind her, "and you've met Viv."

"Nice to meet you, Kara." Adam nodded and moved over to sit next to Viv, who leaned forward displaying her cleavage and purred, "My pleasure."

Nate leaned closer, his brown eyes looking into Kara's. "Is this your first time on a cruise?"

Kara blushed. "Yes. This is my first time cruising."

When was the last time a handsome man had flirted with her? She couldn't remember. But then she didn't get out enough to meet handsome men. She eyed the muscles of Nate's chest and arms and couldn't look away.

He must be a military man, either a Marine or a Navy Seal, judging from the tattoo of a parachute and a swimmer on the upper part of his right arm. She couldn't see the tattoo on his left bicep clear enough to tell what it was. He carried himself with the air of confidence of a military man.

He ran a hand through his dark hair and his bicep flexed. "This is my first time on a cruise too."

His deep and resonating voice made her want to melt.

Three other men joined them, and Nate moved closer to Kara, his muscular arm across the hot tub behind her, now close enough to touch as everyone scooted around, filling the tub. He put off heat and protectiveness from his body.

There was just something about him that made her unable to look away.

"Where are you from, sweetheart?"

*Sweetheart. No one had ever called her sweetheart before. But maybe he was one of those men who called every woman he met sweetheart.*

"Columbus, Ohio."

"A Midwestern gal. I've been there. Clean city. Cold in the winter though."

"Yes. Very. It's nice to get away from the snow."

With those broad shoulders and well-toned body, Nate defined the term "rugged male." Sitting beside him made her feel fragile and yet safe and protected at the same time.

Nate's arm touching Kara's bare shoulders sent tingles down her spine. She slid down into the water until she was submerged to her chin, hoping the water would hide the telltale signs of the way he affected her.

He grinned and glanced down at her swimsuit as if he knew.

She tried to edge forward, but the slanted seat of the hot tub forced her to slide back again. As she bumped into Nate, their thighs touching, she shot him a sideways glance.

*Did his grin deepen?*

He cleared his throat. "So Viv said you won this cruise?"

"Yes." She could barely breathe, let alone answer. Her face flushed as the hot tub grew even warmer.

*He was way too handsome and way too close.*

Her pulse thundered. Maybe she'd stayed in the hot tub too long and her blood pressure had risen.

Maybe she should get out and cool down.

*How long had they been in here?* She'd lost all sense of time.

His brown eyes held an intensity that bathed her in admiration as he watched her. If she'd wanted to fool herself, she could've imagined she was the center of his world, at least for tonight.

"What did you do to win it?"

She glanced at his muscular chest above the bubbling waters, flustered by the intensity of his gaze, yet something pulled her to him as if drawn by an unseen hand. She caught herself before her glance drifted further down his body and her eyes met his again.

He waited for her to answer, watching her.

"I worked a lot of overtime," she said. "I haven't taken a vacation in almost two years."

His eyes softened. "Sounds like you're overdue."

"Yes. Long overdue."

"We have to go clean up for dinner," Viv interrupted.

"I hope my bags have arrived," Kara said.

Adam said, "They haven't delivered all the bags yet.

Some of them are still down below decks being sorted. That's why they never have a formal evening the first night of a cruise. Everyone won't have all their bags delivered by then. If yours have made it to the ship, you may still have a chance they'll deliver them tonight."

Viv leaned closer to Adam. "How do you know so much about cruises?"

"I'm a travel agent, specializing in adventure travel."

"Sounds fascinating." Viv placed her hand on his thigh, no longer in a hurry to go.

*Never the least bit shy, that was Viv. But what had happened to the British boyfriend she'd seemed so head over heels about?*

"I have to take a certain number of cruises a year to keep up my certifications. This year I invited my cousin."

Viv smiled a Cheshire cat grin. "We're glad you did."

Kara suspected Viv was thinking something along the lines of *one hunky man for me and one for my sad friend Kara.*

Viv stood. "Well, we have to be going now."

Right on cue everyone turned to her and their gazes followed her as she stepped out of the tub.

"Hot cha cha," one man said.

Though she didn't respond, Viv's swaying hips were a dead giveaway she was aware of the attention and enjoying every minute. She loved parading in front of men.

Kara followed Viv and reached for her towel on the lounge chair. Ocean breezes blew cooling night air that made her shiver and gave her goose bumps before she wrapped the towel around her.

"See you around, sweetheart," Nate's low voice rasped, creating even more goose bumps that had nothing to do with the cool air. "Hope your luggage turns up."

"Bye." She used the towel to dry herself and then pulled on the sarong, aware of Nate watching her.

*Trouble. This is happening too fast. I'd best stay away from Nate Cooper and that hot tub or I'll be in real hot water.*

NATE WATCHED the women walk away. Both were good-looking. Dark haired Viv was full of fire and blonde Kara was cool, quiet, and curvy.

She'd worn her silky blonde hair tied back in a ponytail tonight and water dripped from the ends. Her long hair had caught his eye first in the airport before he'd gone over to see what was wrong. Then she'd turned her face up to him, pearl complexion heightened with color, green eyes full of panic.

He'd wanted to fix her problem. He'd wanted to

kiss her. And for some reason he'd felt the urge to help her even though he was done rescuing women.

Until Adam suggested this cruise, Nate had been way too busy with work and getting over the last woman who had stung him. Today he found himself thinking of Kara instead of his job. He found himself thinking of a week at sea, playing and enjoying the company of a beautiful woman.

*One who didn't seem the slightest bit interested in chasing and catching him. It was refreshing.*

He'd like to remove the sadness from her eyes and make them sparkle, if she'd let him.

"Hey, Nate," Adam grinned. "I can tip the maître d and make sure the assigned seating assigns Viv and Kara to our table."

"Nice." He threw his head back with a laugh. "Adam, you are a genius."

# CHAPTER THREE

"*O*h baby, did you notice Nate giving you the once over? Twice!" Viv nudged Kara the minute the elevator doors closed.

"He was not."

"Was too."

"And he clearly let Adam know you were off limits."

Kara frowned. "What are you talking about?"

"Didn't you notice how quick he slid his arm around you? That's a man marking territory."

"He did not have his arm around me. It was on the back of the hot tub."

"Right behind you. Or did you not notice?"

"I noticed." Kara shivered. "Cold in here, isn't it?"

"You can have the first shower if you promise not to be too long."

Kara frowned. "I don't take long showers."

"Well, you might after sitting next to that hunk of a man." Viv laughed.

"Viv, would you give it a rest?"

"I won't say another word." Viv started humming. She continued to hum all the way down the hall and into their cabin. When she opened the door she said, "Kara, someone sent flowers!"

"Oh, how pretty!" Kara hurried inside. "Is there a card?"

"Yes." Viv handed it over. "With your name on it."

Kara took the envelope and opened it.

"Well, what does it say?" Viv crossed her arms, impatient.

"Missing you already. Wishing you a great cruise." Kara flipped the card over, puzzled. "No signature."

"That's odd," Viv said. "You'd think they'd want to take credit for sending them. Who do you think sent them?"

"I have no idea. They're pretty though."

"Well, thank you mystery man. Hey, maybe it's Nate."

"I doubt that. We just met."

"Well, I still say you made a conquest. He can't take his eyes off of you."

"The next time we see him, he'll probably be flirting with someone else."

"Not the way he looks at you."

"I wish my luggage was here," Kara said,

changing the subject as she peered out the door, hoping it had arrived.

*No such luck.*

She sighed. "Guess I'll need to borrow a dress after all."

"Here are two to choose from." Viv laid them on the bed. "I'm first in the shower while you decide."

"Okay." She eyed the two cocktail dresses before trying them on. The orange was not her color, though it wasn't as skimpy as the aqua, it was much shorter. She'd hardly be able to sit down in that one. She tried on the aqua and hoped it'd fit.

Viv emerged from her shower. "Nate is so hot. Did you see his military tats? There's nothing sexier than a Marine. Hoo rah."

*She's still talking about him? Has she had him on her mind all this time?* If Viv hadn't latched on to Adam so quick, Kara would've thought Viv had a thing for Nate the way she went on about him.

"What happened to that British guy you were seeing? I thought you really liked him."

"I did. But he's too far away. Long distance relationships never work." Viv shrugged. "I broke it off with him two days ago."

"You never mentioned it."

"It wasn't a big deal. Now about Nate. Travel hook ups are perfect. If you don't click with the guy, you get off the ship and never see him again. You need to get back into dating. And girl, that man is hot, hot, hot."

*Hook ups. Viv always acted like it was all fun and no one got hurt. But how did you let someone get so close to you, so intimate, without feeling something?*

*And if no one got hurt, why did Viv go shopping every time one of her hook ups didn't turn into something more?*

"I'm not looking for a hook up, Viv. I just want to enjoy the sun, the beach, and the water. Relax a little."

"Well, at least tell me you'll try. If a shipboard romance happens, go with the flow."

"I'll go with the flow if it feels right." She wasn't looking for a shipboard romance. If she fell in love, she could have her heart broken. Again. "Okay, you're done in there? Because I really need a shower."

"Yeah, I'm done." Viv dumped out her cosmetic bag on the table in front of the mirror and sat down to put on her makeup. "Go for it."

The shower was small, barely enough room to turn, but the water pressure felt great. Kara closed her eyes and tried to just enjoy it. The soap and shampoo was coconut scented.

*Caribbean here I come.*

When Kara entered the room Viv said, "Which dress did you decide on?"

"The aqua."

"That color will be good on you."

"I hope." She stepped into the thin silk dress she'd borrowed from Viv and turned around. "Zip me?"

"Sure."

Viv zipped the dress. Kara turned around.

"Wow," Viv said. "I'm jealous. You look even better in that dress than I do."

"I do?" Kara tugged at the low cut scooped neck-line and then smoothed her hands down her thighs, wishing the dress covered more skin.

*This is so different from what I'm used to wearing.* Kara had a strict dress code at the bank, so she usually bought conservative dresses. *But maybe different is good.*

She turned in front of the mirror watching the silk move, the dress smooth against her curves. *Oh, this dress feels soft. Sensual. Daring. There'd be no dessert tonight, not wearing this dress. And no crossing these pale legs.*

"Thanks for loaning me the dress."

"That's what mates are for."

Viv may have been done with her British boyfriend but he'd rubbed off on her enough her language had changed. It was hard to get used to.

As Vivian ran a quick comb through her hair, Kara smiled. "Hey, Viv. Remember when we had sleepovers as girls? My mother would braid my hair while you'd hop from one foot to the other, impatient to go out and play?"

"Yeah. I always wondered why your hair took so long."

"I have Mother's thin, slippery hair, though it's not dark."

"Like golden silk, your mother used to say."

They both grew silent, remembering Kara's mother, who had died in a car accident. Viv had been the one who'd stayed with Kara, combing Kara's hair and handing out hugs and Kleenex. It was Kara's senior year of high school and the two became inseparable, where before Viv had been too busy being a cheerleader and going to parties as their friendship drifted. But after the funeral she'd made a real effort to include Kara and helped Kara stop feeling sorry for herself.

"Well." Viv tossed the comb on the dresser, never one to be sentimental for long. "You ready?" She picked up the room card and waved it. "This is all we need. Come on."

Kara slipped on sandals and picked up the little folding map of the ship. "We'll need this so we don't get lost."

"If we get lost, we'll keep going." She laughed. "You can't stay lost on a ship."

"It's a big ship."

"Then take the blimey thing if it'll make you feel better. Come on, I'm starving."

Using the map, Kara found the way to the dining room, where the waiter seated them.

"I hope cruise cuisine is as fantastic as Daryl says it is," she said.

"How would he know? You said he'd never taken a cruise."

"He hasn't."

"The man can't be an expert on everything. But he's the type who thinks he is."

Viv was right about that one, but Kara didn't want to think about her boss right now. She needed this vacation.

The waiter lifted a napkin from her plate with a flourish and placed it in her lap.

"This is dining in style," Viv said as he handed them menus. "Very elegant."

Kara glanced around the dining room.

*Elegant was putting it mildly.*

Crystal chandeliers hung from the ceiling. The furniture and a great wall of mirrors reminded her of the palace at Versailles she'd seen on the History Channel.

She peered over the menu as the waiter seated more passengers at their table. An attractive gray-haired couple sat across from her, and to Viv's right sat a young couple, clearly in love.

Kara looked back down at her menu, hiding her thoughts. Sometimes it was hard to watch couples so deeply in love. It reminded her of her loss and her longings.

"Hello again."

She glanced up. Nate Cooper stood next to her, gazing down into her eyes. He appeared even taller in black pants and a dark red shirt.

"Hello," she said as he sat beside her.

*He's way too handsome, and probably used to women falling all over him.*

*And yet ... he's at my table tonight. Could this be fate?*

"I'm starving. We boarded too late for the lunch buffet," Nate sat back while the waiter placed the napkin in his lap.

"We did too."

She returned to the menu before she said or did something to let him know how off balance he made her feel.

She read the menu three times and still didn't remember what it said.

*How was it possible he looked even more handsome dressed for dinner than he did in swim trunks?*

Having seen his bare chest, she knew what those muscles looked like beneath his shirt. The simple act of him sitting beside her sent warmth coursing through her body.

He reached for his water glass. "Tough decision, isn't it?"

"Yes, it is."

*He had no idea.*

She tried to concentrate again on her menu. He disrupted her concentration without even trying. His scent heightened her pulse and her breathing quickened. She frowned. There were too many choices and dishes she'd never heard of.

"What are you having?" Viv focused her attention on Nate.

*She doesn't get tongue tied every time a handsome man speaks to her. Why does this happen to me?*

"Everything sounds good," said Adam, who sat by Viv.

Still flustered, Kara ordered asparagus shrimp bisque, shrimp cocktail with Louis dressing, and shrimp fettuccine.

"You must really like shrimp," Nate said.

Without realizing it, she'd just ordered every shrimp dish on the menu. "Shrimp is my favorite. I haven't had it in ages." Eating shrimp felt comfortable and familiar.

"Fine dining hasn't been in the budget for a very long time," she said.

"Then I'm glad you can indulge tonight."

The way he said 'indulge' made her toes want to curl.

*How will I ever be able to eat?*

She was aware of each movement he made no matter how small. He'd flustered her, and butterflies flitted about in her now growling belly.

"Excellent choices," the waiter said. He turned to Nate to take his order.

"I'll have the caviar, shrimp cocktail, crayfish salad, swordfish and a baked potato."

Listening to his deep voice rumble made her want to close her eyes.

*If he sounds that good just ordering dinner, what would he sound like whispering sweet nothings?* She reached for her water and nearly knocked her wine glass over. *What's wrong with me? I need to focus on something else.*

Once the waiter had gone, introductions passed around the table. Viv did most of the talking.

Just when Kara gathered the nerve to say something to Nate so he wouldn't think her a complete lump, his caviar arrived. He scooped up the shiny black eggs with his cracker.

*Disgusting. How could he eat that?*

His lips closed over the cracker, and he winked at her.

"Mmm," he rumbled from his throat then swallowed.

His eyes brightened with merriment, and she realized she'd been staring. Her cheeks warmed, and she reached for her wine glass.

"Would you like some?" he offered with a smile. "It's delicious."

"No. No, thank you." She shook her head.

"I'll try anything once. Can't know if I like it until

I do." He winked again, and her knees weakened. "Be adventurous."

"Ha," Viv laughed. "You're barking up the wrong tree. Kara's not the adventurous type."

"All the more reason to try." His brown eyes dared her.

"Go on, Kara, it won't kill you," Viv said.

Nate scooped a cracker into the black goop and held it out to her. "Come on sweetheart, give it a try."

Mesmerized, she opened her mouth like a bird and let him slide it in. Her pulse accelerated from the simple act. Something seemed so sensual about it and her face flushed at the thought. The caviar tasted of salt and of the sea. She swallowed it down fast then took a drink of water.

"Well?" His mouth twitched with amusement.

Everyone at the table watched her. She'd become the center of attention. Heat crept up her cheeks. "It's okay."

Nate laughed.

She turned to her first course and stared at the soup, a green liquid, where pink shrimp floated. Taking a spoonful she sipped.

*Whoever thought of cold soup? Oh, it's pretty good.*

She finished her soup and sat waiting for the next course while Viv chattered like a magpie.

"The day at the private island should be fun." Viv focused her attention on Adam and then Nate. "Do you know if they allow topless sunbathing?"

Kara watched Nate for his reaction. His expression was remote, unreadable. He caught her gaze and smiled.

Adam cleared his throat. "I don't know, but if you want privacy on the beach that might be arranged."

"Is that so?" The older man at their table got a gleam in his eye. "We're celebrating our fiftieth wedding anniversary this week." He placed his hand over his wife's. "Perhaps we could hold the renewal of vows there privately instead of on board. It would be much more intimate."

"William McKay," his wife said. "Don't even think about it." She pushed her chair back and stood. "Topless beaches. Hmph. All he thinks about is naked women." She stalked from the room.

"Excuse me." He stood to go after her. "Darling, please wait for me."

Everyone at the table laughed, especially the two newlyweds.

"We've arranged for private dining in our cabin all of the other nights," the new bridegroom said. "So you won't be seeing us after dinner tonight."

His new bride giggled. "It's been lovely to meet you all."

"Likewise." Nate said. "And congratulations."

"Yes, congratulations," Kara said. Adam and Viv chimed in too.

"Well," Viv said after the newlywed couple had

left. "I didn't know the mention of topless beaches would scare everyone off."

"I don't think it did," Kara said. "I'm sure they'd already planned their honeymoon prior to meeting you."

*Everything is not always about you.*

She focused her attention back on Nate.

*What did he do for a living? From his tanned muscular body it must be something outdoors, something active.*

"So, Nate, what do you do?"

"I'm a scuba dive instructor."

"Oh my."

"Kara can barely swim," Viv said. "She's phobic."

*Well thank you, Viv. First you tell him all about how I'm now widow when we've barely net the man and now you tell him all about how I'm phobic.*

Kara wanted to dive under the table.

"I've taught many people how to swim. I could teach you."

"Oh, I, I don't know."

Adam saved her by changing the subject. "Are you going to the show tonight?"

"No, we're going shopping," Viv said. "Kara's luggage never came and the shops didn't open until we sailed."

Kara placed her napkin on the table. "We'd better go."

Nate held Kara's chair as she stood to join Viv.

"Thank you." Kara was still embarrassed and tongue tied around Nate, but she hadn't forgotten her manners.

"Good night."

She felt Nate's warm gaze follow her as she walked away, the silk brushing across her body, making her aware of every movement, caressing her skin.

"Wait till we finish shopping," Viv said. "You'll look so good; Nate will want to eat you up."

The thought of his lips against her skin made Kara shiver.

Viv laughed. "I know someone who's having naughty thoughts."

"What if I am? I could listen to him talk all night. That voice..."

"Mmm hmm." Viv nodded. "I would do more than listen. Nate is one sexy hunk of a man."

"If I *was* looking for a man, and I am *not*," Kara said, as they passed two jewelry boutiques, "a scuba dive instructor would not be on my list. That's a dangerous job."

Viv paused in front of the tux rental shop. "Picture him in this," she tapped on the window in front of a black tux. "Or better yet, picture him taking it off, just for you, slow, one piece at a time."

Kara froze, the image clear in her mind. "Hmmm." She moved on past the liquor store, away from the tuxes and dangerous thoughts.

Viv laughed as she followed. "You have steamy thoughts of him; you want to see him naked."

Her singsong voice rankled.

*She could be so exasperating.*

"I do not."

She hadn't thought of it until Vivian brought it up. But now the visual image wouldn't go away. So maybe she hadn't been thinking of seeing him naked a few minutes ago, but now...

*Maybe he'd wear a tux on formal night to the Captain's Dinner. It wouldn't hurt to make another small wish ... to dance under the stars with him.*

# CHAPTER FOUR

*V*iv held up two swimsuits. A flashy silver one and a white one that would turn transparent when wet.

"I can't wear either one of those," Kara said. "I'd scare the fish."

Viv rolled her eyes. "Listen, you can get the ultimate tan on a trip like this and the best way to get one short of tanning topless is to get the smallest swimsuit possible."

"I'm not tanning topless."

"Yeah, you're too shy. That's why you need one of these."

Kara sighed and turned back to the racks. "Why does shopping for a swimsuit have to be such an ordeal?"

"It doesn't have to be. It can be fun if you let it."

"I don't see how this can ever be fun."

Viv laughed. "Think about it. What if you snuck your boyfriend in to help you in and out of them?"

"Viv, you didn't!"

Viv laughed and winked.

*Viv always did think up the wildest things. We had such fun in high school. When did my life become so serious I stopped having fun?*

Kara reached for a red bikini with little white daisies on it that tied at the hips. "I'm going to try this one."

"All right Daisy Mae." Viv smiled. "Go try it on."

When Kara tried it on she couldn't believe her luck.

She looked in the mirror. *Wow. Is that really me?*

The red bikini fit like it was made for her, nothing to pull at or tug on and it emphasized her curves.

She liked it. She liked it very much.

When she emerged, Viv was still looking through the racks.

"I'm getting this one."

"Really?"

Viv's surprised expression made Kara smile. "Yes, really."

Kara found a dress she liked and hurried to make her purchases since the shops were closing.

On the next floor they passed a shop with the prettiest gold sandals Kara had ever seen in the shop window. "I'll bet those are expensive."

"They'd go with everything. Elegant." Viv yawned. "Too bad the shops are closed. Hey girl, do you want to go clubbing?"

"Not tonight. I'm tired and you're yawning."

"A little coffee and I'd be good to go."

This would probably be the only night Viv didn't stay up dancing until dawn. Her favorite thing to do.

"We have the rest of the week," Kara said.

"Righto. You look knackered."

"What?"

"Tired."

"Oh. Yes, I am."

When Viv opened the cabin door the lights were dimmed. She took one step inside then jumped back into Kara. "Quick, turn on the light."

Kara flicked the switch. "Oh, look, swans."

Their cabin steward had made swans out of white towels. One sat on each bed beside a chocolate mint.

Viv sunk onto her bed. "I thought it was a snake."

"The curved head does resemble a snake." Kara smiled. Viv was afraid of snakes.

"I can't believe I let a towel frighten me."

"I won't tell." Kara turned around. "Help me out of this dress. I'll send it to the ship's dry cleaner tomorrow."

"Okay." Viv unzipped the dress.

The dry cleaning fees were higher here but Viv had planned to wear that dress one night. Kara had been careful with her money to have enough for some extras on this trip.

After liquidating her husband's subcontracting business and paying his creditors, Kara had barely enough to pay her monthly bills. He'd cashed in his life insurance to pay off part of his business debts and left her with nothing except their house and mortgage.

But now she had her head above water again.

She couldn't remember when she'd last splurged on anything fun. She was long overdue. When was the last time she bought a new dress?

"What do you want to do tomorrow?" Viv asked.

"Lounge in the sun, sip a frosty drink."

"Sounds good." Viv stepped into the bathroom.

Kara changed into the shorts and tee shirt she'd worn at the airport. She flipped through the TV programs while waiting for Viv to come out. The ship had a shopping channel, a weather channel, an excursion channel, and a movie channel playing *Jaws*. Then she remembered she never called Daryl back. She walked to the safe and took out her phone.

Turning it on she saw four calls and five texts from him. She dialed his number.

"Kara," he answered on the first ring. "It's about time you called me."

"What's wrong?"

"I've been worried about you."

"I'm fine. The uh, ship's reception isn't very good."

"Did you get my flowers?"

"Oh." Her heart sunk. "Yes. Thank you."

*Of course they weren't from Nate. What was she thinking?*

"Kara?"

"Yes?"

"I thought I'd lost you." He sounded relieved.

"I can still hear you."

"Did they find your luggage?"

"Not yet."

"Go shopping. I'll wire you money."

"Thank you, but I'm fine. I bought a few things tonight."

"I'll treat you."

"No, Daryl."

"Listen to me. Take the money."

But she didn't want to listen to him trying to push her into something she didn't want. "Daryl, can you hear me? We're losing the connection. I will talk to you later. Bye."

"Kara? Damn it."

She heard the frustration in his voice. Turning off the phone gave her such relief.

*Why was he being so pushy?*

Just because he'd advised her in the months since her husband died didn't mean she had to follow all his advice about money. Though she was grateful he'd helped her straighten out the mess Neil had left her with, which was an accountant's nightmare, there were days when she wished he didn't know any of her personal business and other days when she felt guilty for even thinking that after how supportive he'd been.

She locked the phone up in the safe just before Viv came out of the bathroom. "Were you talking to someone? Oh, I don't believe it. *Jaws* is playing?"

"I've been flipping channels." Kara switched off the TV. "Someone must have a morbid sense of humor."

"Yeah. Twisted."

Kara took her turn in the bathroom. When she came out, Vivian's snores greeted her.

*She's such a heavy sleeper she'd sleep through a fire alarm. ... No, don't think about fires or sharks. This cruise is supposed to be fun.*

She flipped through the TV channels, finding nothing to catch her interest. The phone call had left her feeling agitated instead of sleepy so she decided to stretch her legs. She slipped the map into the pocket of her shorts and left the room, heading for the pool deck.

She entered the open middle deck where the outdoor pool stood empty and climbed the steps to the upper deck, wondering how the sea would look at night. The damp rail against her hand hinted of dew covering every surface. The air held a chill.

Kara leaned against the inner rail and looked up at the moon, partially hidden behind clouds.

*No stars out tonight. Not that it matters. Stargazing is for lovers. This is when it hurts the most. This lonely time when night descends and lovers curl up to sleep in comfortable companionship. When I'm unable to sleep and wander alone in the night. Oh, how I wish...*

She closed her eyes and held her breath as she sent wishes into the night. *I wish this loneliness would go away and never return again. I wish I never had to spend another lonely night wandering sleepless and unable to sleep.*

When she opened them again, the vast dark of night spread around her. Dark sky and water surrounding the boat erased any sense of a horizon. She could see no edge, no order. There was only this boat and the half-hidden moon to bear witness to her loneliness.

The open decks now stood almost empty. One couple strolled hand in hand on the deck beneath her, and the bartender below wiped down his bar for tomorrow.

No one stood nearby to save her if she fell over the rail. It reached almost to her shoulders so the possibility remained slim, and she wasn't standing near enough to the outer rail to fall but still...

*If I fell in who would know? There were news reports of people vanishing off ships. It would be morning before anyone even started looking for me. The deep, dark ocean could swallow me whole, as if I were a grain of sand. My God.*

Kara shivered and wrapped her arms about herself.

*If only wishes did come true.*

How she'd grown to dislike the night. She had no one to talk to, no tasks to take her mind off dark thoughts. She wondered what Nate was doing tonight.

*He was probably sound asleep like Viv.*

Kara wrapped her arms around herself and shivered.

"Nights at sea can be chilly," Nate said and she jumped, turning toward him eyes wide.

"Here, sweetheart." He held out his jacket and stepped in front of her. "This will keep you warm."

Kara blinked. "Oh, no, I couldn't."

"I don't mind." He offered her a smile. "In fact, I insist."

Goose bumps covered her arms.

"You're cold." He placed his jacket around her shoulders.

She let him drape the jacket over her shoulders and looked up into his deep brown eyes, her breath catching.

His hands lingered on her shoulders and he gazed down at her upturned face. As he searched her eyes, she wondered if he would kiss her.

His gaze lit on her lips.

Her lips trembled.

"You're still cold," he said. He ran his hands up and down her arms, warming her.

"Thank you."

"My pleasure." He smiled. "Better now?"

"Yes."

He moved to stand beside her.

Wind blew a strand of her long blonde hair across her face, and she pushed it back with her other hand. The silence stretched as the moon shone above them and the ship moved through the dark sea.

"It's so deep and dark out there. Dangerous."

"There's nothing to be afraid of, Kara. You're safe here."

"If the ship were to sink..."

"You would be safe in your life jacket in the boat assigned to your muster station."

"If I made it to the boat in time."

He turned her around to face him and looked into her eyes. "I would find you."

She gazed up at him, her eyes searching his.

"I'd see that you made it into the boat. But tonight the boat is not sinking. Everything is fine. You're fine. There's no reason to be afraid."

She looked back out at the dark water. "It feels as if we're the only people on the ship right now, doesn't it?"

"There's a whole crew working behind the scenes

to make all this happen." He guided her to the inside rail and pointed to the bartender below who'd just hung up the deck phone. "There are plenty of people about keeping an eye on the passengers." He moved closer to her.

Kara's pulse quickened as his lithe body moved beside her. His jacket around her shoulders felt like a warm hug, and the comfort of his hand on her back made her wish he would hold her close, chasing her fears away. Yet they'd just met, and the intensity of what she felt, despite that fact, scared her.

For a moment she'd thought he'd kiss her, but maybe she imagined it. Maybe she imagined it because it had been so long since someone kissed her.

She moved beside him and glanced where he'd pointed. A man rolled a cart of liquor out of the elevator and over to the bar. The bartender began to restock supplies while a deck hand mopped the floor in front of the bar.

As Nate stood next to her in silence, the night breeze bathed her in the scent of his cologne, filling her senses.

*He smelled so good.*

"There are hundreds of people on this ship you'll never see," his low voice rumbled.

*Oh, that voice.* She could listen to him all night long.

"You're not as alone as you think."

*How can he read me so well? I just met him. Yet somehow he doesn't feel like a stranger. I feel so comfortable standing here beside him.*

"I'm glad. I wouldn't want to be alone, out here."

She watched his strong shoulders as the wind blew against his shirt. *Now he was probably cold.*

"I should give your jacket back. It's chilly out here."

"No, sweetheart, I'm just fine."

He gazed into her eyes and she looked back into his deep brown eyes, losing all sense of time, or moments sped up or slowed down. There was only his gaze and his hand on her back, his warmth surrounding her.

Somehow she felt calm and nervous all at once. Butterflies flitted in her stomach.

He was attentive. She wasn't used to that quiet attentiveness or the way he gazed into her eyes...

"I'm afraid of deep water." The words spilled out before she could call them back.

"Yes, I know." His hand, warm and comforting, continued rubbing her back. "And yet, there you were, on the top deck by the rails when the ocean is pitch black at night. You're a brave woman, Kara Worth, to face your fear."

"Oh, I don't know about that."

"Well, I do."

"Yes, I guess you would, with your job."

If she were looking for a man, she wouldn't choose one who faced danger daily by diving into the bottom of the ocean. But she wasn't looking. She wasn't.

"It's slick out here." Nate ran his hand across the rail then rubbed it down his slacks. "From the sea." He inhaled deep as if enjoying the night air and squinted off into the distance. "We're moving at a good clip. Some passengers might get seasick if we moved this fast during the day. The ship travels faster when they retract the stabilizers. But it can also rock the passengers to sleep."

His voice rolled over her like a warm breeze. Now she noticed the rocking of the ship on the sea.

"Well, good," she said, "Because I have trouble sleeping." It wasn't like her to share so much of herself with someone she barely knew. He'd know her whole life story if she kept this up.

"What do you do for insomnia?" he asked.

"Usually I get up and move about. Do something. Then try going back to sleep."

*Great. Now he'd give her all sorts of manly advice as if he could cure her problems. Like Neil used to do. Sometimes a woman just needed someone to listen.*

"You and I have something in common," he said. "I usually go for a walk. Like tonight."

"Oh. That's good." *Brilliant, Kara. He'll be swept away by your intelligent conversation as well as the boatload of fear you have.*

He smiled at her. "Want to walk around the deck with me?"

"Sure." She was unaccustomed to companionship during the evenings when the night terrors struck. Maybe after a stroll around the deck, she'd be able to sleep tonight.

She pulled her long, blonde hair out from under the jacket and he watched it slide loose as an easy smile played at the corners of his mouth.

They walked for a minute in silence. Her foot skidded, and he caught her elbow, his hand warm and strong.

"Careful, sweetheart. The wind picks up as we near the bow." He left his hand on her elbow to guide her.

His touch comforted and created a stirring deep within her. She shivered as an ocean breeze blew across the deck.

Nate's touch struck a vibrant chord inside that had been silent for what seemed forever. Now the chord hummed low and slow beneath the calm front she presented to the world.

*Could he tell what his touch was doing?*

The thought made her flush.

A salty breeze blew and another shiver ran down her spine.

*Oh, these shivers are more than the night air.*

She'd never responded like this even to Neil. This was beyond anything she'd ever experienced.

Nate called her sweetheart. *What would it be like to be his sweetheart?* To hear the endearment every day and know he loved and cared for her?

But she couldn't fall for Nate.

*It would be far too easy. It would hurt too much.*

She had to stay away from Nate Cooper before her emotions got out of hand. Before the craving to be held and loved made her do something she'd regret. Before she fell fast and hard and could no longer tell what was real and what was her craving creating something that wasn't real and lasting.

He halted. "We can go in if you're cold." He stepped close and pulled his jacket tighter around her shoulders. His brown eyes gazed into hers. "I know a quiet corner where we can get a cup of cappuccino."

"All right," she agreed. It was late. And she should go. But something inside of her didn't want to say good night. Didn't want to say goodbye to him.

*Yes, better to go in where there were other people.*

As long as they weren't alone, as long as someone else was there, she wouldn't lose herself to this humming. She wouldn't lose her heart only to have it broken again.

She'd just met him. As comfortable as it felt to be here with him, Nate was still a stranger.

Nate led her back to the stairs, holding her elbow all the way down. He was right about the slick decks and she didn't want to fall.

He made her feel cared for, looked after. Warmth flowed through her while his steady touch sent a light sensation up her arm as each of her senses came alive. How could he make her feel comforted and nervous at the same time?

By the time they reached the bottom of the stairs she was breathless, light headed.

She wanted to run. She wanted to stay here like this forever.

## CHAPTER FIVE

$\mathcal{N}$ate placed his palm on the small of Kara's back and guided her to a piano bar, where a bored bartender leaned on the counter. The man, whose gold name badge read "Mario, Italy," straightened.

"No customers this late, Mario?" Nate pulled out a chair for Kara and she sat.

"No, sir."

"How about two cappuccinos to warm up two night owls?"

"Coming right up."

Mario added a pinch of something to the steaming liquid and placed a cup in front of each of them. "I make it a just so for you." He held his thumb and finger together as he waved his hand. "You try it."

*Italians were so expressive.*

Kara sipped and smiled. "It's delicious."

Satisfied, he nodded then returned to the bar.

Nate sampled his. "It is good." He leaned back in his chair, "So, Kara, what's your favorite place in the world to visit?"

"I haven't been far."

"Your most memorable trip then."

"Washington D.C."

"That's a happening city. What did you do there?"

"We saw the Lincoln Memorial, the Smithsonian, and the zoo."

"We?"

"My husband, Neil, and I."

"Viv told me what happened. I'm sorry for your loss."

"Thank you." Kara looked down into her coffee mug. "He was shot at a gas station while filling up our car. I was waiting in the car. We were on our way back from Washington. The police determined it was a random act of violence. They never found out who did it."

"How long ago did this happen?"

She lifted her head and gazed back at him. "A year and a half."

He searched her eyes and was silent for a moment. "That's a hard thing to go through."

"Yes." She nodded.

"I understand. I lost several good men during battle."

"You were in the military?"

"Yes. Marine Recon."

"Thank you for your service."

He smiled. "You're welcome."

"Is that where you got your tattoos?"

"Yes."

Kara had noticed he had tattoos, one on each arm, but hadn't looked too close at them. Being near him in the hot tub had made her feel too shy to do more than glance at his tattoos.

"What do they stand for? I saw the parachute but couldn't see the one on your left."

"On my left is the Marine Corps eagle, globe, and anchor, and my other one is for Recon with the parachute and scuba diver."

"So you know what it is to be shot at."

"Yes."

She looked down at her cup. "For a long time after my husband was shot I had terrible nightmares. Like I was seeing it happening again right in front of me and then I'd wake in a sweat."

She'd shared herself with him again so easily as if she'd known him forever. What would he think of her?

"That's normal." Nate nodded.

*He actually understood. On a level no one else did.* Unlike her friends, he didn't say get over it or treat her with pity. Instead, he acted normal. And that felt really good.

"Normal."

"Yes."

He was the first person she'd met who'd heard her story and treated it matter-of-factly without the usual poor Kara attitude. She wanted to move on with her life, but how could she when everywhere she went everyone treated her like poor Kara? Viv was the worst.

*Normal. Amazing how a simple ordinary word could feel so good.*

Nate patiently waited for her to speak. Something else she wasn't used to.

"I try to remember the good parts of our trip more than what happened after."

"I understand. Is this your first trip since Washington?"

"Yes."

"Well, I hope you have fun. It sounds like you're overdue."

"Yes, I guess I am." She smiled. "I'm looking forward to the private island."

"What are you planning to do there?"

"Oh, just lounge on the beach with a book."

"Have you ever been snorkeling?"

"No."

"I'd be happy to teach you."

"Oh, I don't know." She hesitated. "I only recently learned how to swim."

"You'll be fine, sweetheart. You'll wear an inflatable vest, and I'll make sure nothing happens to you."

"Well, maybe. But I'm not a very good swimmer."

"You don't have to be. You just float and hold my hand."

"Oh. Okay, I can do that."

"Good." He smiled. "You're going to love it. All the brightly colored fish and the coral. It's a beautiful world down there. I'm looking forward to showing it to you."

Kara listened as Nate described places he'd gone snorkeling and scuba diving. He had traveled all over the world.

His confidence and physical strength comforted her. Perhaps that was why she didn't hesitate to share private things with him. He seemed like a long lost friend. Familiar and safe.

Time seemed to stop when he was near, as if they were in a dream on some other plain. One where she belonged. Where she was destined to be.

*This isn't logical. This is real life, not a dream.*

She pushed her thoughts away and finished her drink.

After she finished, Nate slipped his fingers beneath hers. "I've enjoyed getting to know you better, Kara." His thumbs rubbed the back of her hands. "Thank you for sharing what was troubling you tonight."

Kara blushed.

His gaze held such warmth and tenderness she felt lost within it. Lost and yet found.

"Walk you to your cabin?"

"I'd like that."

"Good."

On the way, they examined the art covering the walls throughout the ship. He knew something of art and though she knew little, he told her she had a good eye.

"I always wanted to paint or draw," Kara said.

"What stopped you?"

"Oh, I don't know."

She'd put away her scribbling when she married Neil to focus on their marriage. Neil wasn't much into artsy things and never understood her "doodles," as he called them.

Maybe she'd take a class when she got back home. Just for fun. Maybe sketch a thing or two. It had been years since she'd thought of doing that.

Somehow she didn't think Nate would find it silly. Still she said nothing of what she was thinking.

They started down the hall toward her stateroom. Something sat outside her door.

"Oh, look," she said. "That could be my luggage."

"I'll bet it is."

They stopped outside the cabin door, and she checked the luggage tags to be sure. "Yes." She sighed with relief. "Oh, good."

"I'm glad. Now you can rest without worrying and get a good night's sleep."

She smiled. "I hope so."

He picked up one of her bags and waited as she opened the door. The sound of Viv's snoring greeted them. They smiled at each other then he set the bag inside for her.

The cabin steward came around the corner carrying an extra blanket. "I can get those for you in a moment," he said.

"Thanks, I've got them." Nate lifted the other.

The steward nodded, moving away to knock on another door, it opened and he handed the occupant the blanket.

Once Nate set the bags inside her room, his hand caught hers. He pulled her closer, letting the door close.

He leaned in as she looked up, the smile still hovering on her lips.

*He's going to kiss me.*

Butterflies flitted in her stomach as his lips descended and brushed hers, touching hers like a whisper.

Like the whisper of a wish made in the dark of night.

Raising his mouth from hers he gazed into her eyes. "Good night sweetheart," he whispered. "Sweet dreams."

"Good night," she breathed, her lips tingling from

his kiss. Still feeling she was within a dream, she opened the door again for him to step outside, and then she eased it closed. She leaned against it on the other side and pressed her fingers to her lips.

*Just one kiss. A gentle whisper of a kiss.*

A soft kiss that made her wish for more. So much more. But it was just a kiss.

She told herself that as she got ready for bed. Repeated it as she climbed into bed and curled up on her side.

*Just a kiss.*

Kara touched her lips with her fingertips. If only he'd kiss her again.

*Once was not enough.*

As she lay in the dark, caught up in the magic of a simple kiss, the magic of a simple wish, there in the dark she sent up another wish. A wish he'd kiss her again tomorrow night and more than once.

Spending time with Nate reminded her of how much she missed having someone in her life and not just someone to talk to. She missed waking in the night and reaching out to touch the man she loved, knowing she wasn't alone.

The small ship's bunk she'd curled up in felt empty even though it was small, though not as empty as her king-sized bed at home.

As the ship rocked her, she lay still, closing her eyes, remembering the sound of Nate's voice, the way his eyes looked into hers and the gentle touch of his lips.

The ship's movements lulled her into sleep. She dreamed. In her dream Nate kissed her over and over.

It was the soundest sleep she'd had in years.

The next morning, as Kara opened the door to their cabin, Viv squinted at her with one eye. "It's too early to get up."

"I've already been to the gym, the cafeteria and the shops. It's not as early as you think."

Viv groaned but sat up. "What did you get?"

"Those gold sandals."

"I ought to get a pair." Viv swung her feet out of bed and lifted the phone. "I'm ordering room service. You hungry?"

*Didn't she hear me say I'd been to the cafeteria? Sometimes I think she doesn't pay attention.*

"No." Kara shook her head. "I've eaten. But I do need a shower."

"Oh hey, there's your luggage. Cool. I didn't hear the room steward bring them in."

Kara started to say Nate had brought them in, but stopped.

*Viv doesn't need to know everything. It's not like she's paying attention anyway.*

"I'm glad they came. Now I can relax," Kara said.

"A day by the pool, that's what you need."

"By the time you get your shower, I'll be ready and we can head up."

Kara waited an hour while Viv fussed over her hair, giving it a few sprays of hairspray and redoing her eye shadow three times as Kara sat flipping through a magazine about the cruise line.

*At this rate it will be lunchtime before we get there. Why is she taking so long? We're only going to the pool.*

Finally Viv placed sunglasses on her head. "Are you ready?"

"I've been ready."

Up on deck, Kara watched the surrounding sea. The sun had turned it a brilliant shade of blue.

*There was so much of it. So very much it seemed to have no end or edge. The ship is far beyond any shoreline. There're no other ships, just this big blue sea.*

Kara felt small and cut off from everything she knew.

*There's only this ship and the people on it, in the middle of this great big, wide ocean.*

"Ladies, would you care for a towel?" An attendant held out a blue and white *Wishing Star* towel for each of them, and then they walked the decks looking for two lounge chairs together.

"Looks like we'd have to get here early to find a good spot," Kara said.

Viv squeezed Kara's arm and pointed. "That woman and child are leaving. Hurry, we'll grab their chairs."

The lounge chairs stood beside the main pool with the waterfall. Kara settled into one, watching the activities director set up a microphone by the pool.

"Hey, girl, front row seats." Viv grinned. "Pool Olympics starts in fifteen minutes."

Male contestants started lining up, and the activities director called for the ladies to join in. None volunteered. The men had well-formed physiques, and each seemed anxious to prove his masculinity to onlookers. Several eyed Kara's red bikini as they strutted past. Each smiled, one winked and flexed his muscles, and a few puffed out their chests.

As Nate walked past, Kara couldn't help but notice the way his powerful, well-muscled body moved with the easy grace of an athlete. He made no extra effort to gain her attention, yet he drew her gaze like a magnet. Kara leaned back in her chair, trying to appear relaxed as she soaked up the sun.

*Yes, he looks good.*

Nate entered the games.

Kara noticed Nate's glance. A part of her reveled in his open admiration. She felt beautiful. It had been a long time since she felt that way.

The first game was a beer-drinking game and consisted of six players lined up on each side of the pool. When the director asked again if any ladies would join in, Nate's gaze locked on hers and she lowered her lashes. She shook her head.

*Silly, overgrown boys. And it's only mid-day.*

After the first contest ended and his team won, Nate scooped water, splashed it on his face, then glanced at her and winked.

She couldn't resist a smile.

The two teams lined up for the second game. The first man in each line had to put on a large T-shirt and swim to the other end of the pool, pulling himself out then eat a cracker, drink a small carton of creamer before blowing up a balloon and swimming back to hand off his T-shirt to the next teammate.

Nate stood tensed to dive into the pool. Damp tendrils of hair curled on his forehead and around his ears. One dark lock fell a little forward onto his head, and he brushed it back with one hand, his muscles rippling.

"He's a fair treat," Viv said, breaking into Kara's thoughts. "That's one solid man."

"Mm hm," was the best Kara could offer in reply. *What was it about the man that turned her brain to mush?*

He bent, poised to dive in for his turn, his quadriceps solid as a rock.

"Ooh," Viv squealed. "How'd you like to wake up next to that bloody great hunk of man every morning?"

"Quiet." Kara's face heated. "He'll hear you."

Nate dove in. As he swam, Kara entertained the

idea Viv had introduced. It would be heaven to have those strong arms around her every night. She'd sleep like a baby.

She watched him drink the creamer. It coated his lips before he wiped it off with the back of his hand. Watching his lips made her swallow hard.

He blew up the balloon, dove in, swam across, and handed off his T-shirt. His team won again. From the look of triumph on his face, she knew he was a man who enjoyed winning.

The third game sounded easier. One contestant from each team would dive into the pool filled with ping-pong balls and then use his swimsuit to store as many balls as he could get his hands on.

"Ladies, are you sure none of you want to join us for this last game?" the activities director coaxed again.

"Come on, Kara." Viv sat up, but Kara pulled her back. "Are you crazy? I can't do that. Everyone will be watching and I'm not sure I remember much from the swimming lessons."

"Right," Viv said. "We have the best view right here anyway."

"Thank you, Viv," Kara leaned back and exhaled.

"No takers?" The man sounded disappointed. "All right, men. Show us if you have enough balls."

Nate laughed then glanced at Kara. He grinned at her and she glanced down.

*No, everything is still where it belongs.*

She tugged at her top and saw her skin was getting pink. The mid-day sun reflected off the water. Once the games ended, she'd move into the shade.

"Let's see if Nate and Adam will catch the show with us after dinner," Viv said.

"Okay." Kara felt giddy at the thought of a whole evening with him. Dinner and a show never sounded so good.

Nate climbed out of the water, water streaming down his muscular body and his swim trunks bulging with ping-pong balls. Kara had to put her hand over her mouth to hide her laugh.

He grinned at her as he pulled the balls out for the activities director to count. Nate's eyes sparkled.

"Girl, that man is hot," Viv said.

Kara couldn't reply.

The hum inside began again. *Oh my. It isn't only his voice and his touch. All he has to do is look over and ... The look in his eyes right now ...*

She gasped. What was wrong with her? She had to get this under control.

"Breathe, girlfriend," Viv said. She pulled a straw hat out of her beach bag and placed it on Kara's head. "Lean back, stay cool, and don't be obvious. You'll scare him off."

"Let it be, Viv," Kara snapped, irritated.

Maybe she was going mad from lack of sex. Viv said it could happen. Kara had never had this problem before. Kara squirmed and hoped she didn't look like she was in heat or something.

The director handed out ribbons and T-shirts; Nate accepted his award then headed toward Kara's chair.

Kara sucked in a deep breath and tried to compose herself, but her poise was only a fragile shell. One more smile, one more touch from this hunk of a man and her peace of mind might well be non-existent, the damage irreversible.

He came closer, his deep brown eyes so intent on her that for a moment she forgot to breathe.

Then he stood at the foot of her lounge chair.

Beneath the warmth of his gaze something deep within her melted, yet she remained frozen, waiting for one word from him, her breath coming shallow while her pulse thundered.

"Hello, sweetheart." His voice held a rasp of excitement.

She ducked her head, shy. "Hello."

He knelt then peeked under her straw hat. His brown eyes met hers. "Care to uh, reward the winner with a kiss?"

She could barely breathe, let alone answer.

# CHAPTER SIX

*N*ate winked to let Kara know he was teasing then laid his newly won T-shirt across her legs. "You may not have a prize for me, sweetheart, but I have one for you." He sat on the lounge chair next to her. "There's no way I can wear a medium, and they're out of large."

"Oh. What?" She was disoriented, her mind on the kiss he'd asked her for.

*Oh. A tee shirt. He's giving me the tee shirt he won.*

"Are you sure?"

His hand closed over her ankle, and he gave it a squeeze. She inhaled at the contact of his warm hand and froze, unable to speak.

"Sweetheart, I'm always sure."

Nate's hand on her skin sent energy shooting all the way up her body. That tingling feeling came over her again and like the other night, she felt torn between wanting to run and wanting to stay. His hand gentle and firm on her ankle anchored her.

Viv piped up. "You guys having dinner in the main dining room tonight?"

"Wouldn't miss it. That's where the best food is." Nate smiled at Kara and his smile combined with the touch of his hand had Kara melting.

"Jolly good," Viv said. "Meet up with us to watch the show afterwards?"

*Jolly good? The British expressions Viv picked up from her latest beau will drive me mad if I have to hear them all week.*

Nate tipped his head in an attempt to catch Kara's full attention, which she noted out of the corner of her eye, but her gaze remained riveted on his fingers. The sight of his long tanned fingers against her pale skin made her stomach flip.

He released her ankle and she exhaled. She longed for him to touch her again.

"It's a date," he replied, his attention directed at Kara. "We could go dancing afterward."

"Yes." She breathed the word and heard herself speak it, before it registered. It wasn't until he'd winked and walked away that she came back to herself.

"Earth to Kara," Viv said. "Girl, you need to get out of the sun."

Back in the room, Kara showered then lay down on the bed to take a nap. But she couldn't relax. Her thoughts wouldn't rest. Thoughts of dancing with Nate and the anticipation of his touch and his kisses filled her with excitement and nervous tension.

Viv came out of the bathroom, combing wet hair, and bent to pick an envelope off the floor. "This has your name on it."

"The cabin steward must have slid it under the door." Kara reached for it and opened it. "Oh, wow."

"What is it?"

"A gift certificate for the spa." Kara frowned when she saw who sent it, but she remained silent.

"Let's get pedicures."

"Pedicures?"

"Hello, earth to Kara. Pay attention." Viv tapped the bottom of Kara's foot with her comb. "Pedicures. You have winter feet."

*What did she mean, winter feet?*

Kara looked down at her feet, which appeared fine. She kept her toenails trimmed.

"I have a Pedi every Thursday." Viv displayed her toes. "Just in time for the weekend."

"I've never had a pedicure before."

"Come on, it'll be fun."

Kara hesitated.

*I won't tell her it's from Daryl unless she asks. I don't want to think about my boss right now or my job. I'm here to relax, not stress over things. Cruises are supposed to be relaxing.*

"Don't be an old stick in the mud. Come on, Kara."

"All right."

Viv chattered away about pedicures and manicures, but never once asked who gave Kara the gift certificate.

They headed to the spa where an attendant gave them a tour.

Viv pointed to the massage chairs. "You get to sit in the massage chair while they do your feet. It's wonderful."

"It's expensive."

Prices in the spa were higher than pedicures advertised back home. But at sea they had no competition.

"All the good spas charge more. It's worth it."

"All right." Kara handed the attendant her gift certificate. "Two pedicures please."

*The pampering would be good. In fact it's long overdue.*

Kara sat and slipped her feet into the bubbling water, closing her eyes. Suddenly an image of Nate's hand closing over her big toe filled her mind. Neil hadn't paid any attention to her toes. She'd stopped painting her toenails years ago. She pondered this while the massage chair rumbled up and down her back, her feet soaking in bubbling water.

She didn't realize she'd dozed off until a hand

touched her shoulder. "Sorry to wake you, miss, but it's time to dry off."

Kara opened her eyes and glanced at Viv who offered her a big "I told you so" smirk.

"This is relaxing. I can't believe I dozed off though."

"Took you long enough to relax."

*If Nate touches my toes again, they'll be baby smooth.*

"Thanks, Viv. I'm glad you suggested this."

"You're welcome."

When they left, Kara's toes were a deep, elegant red.

"Let's both get something new to wear tonight," Viv said.

"Why not?" Kara laughed.

They headed to the stores, Viv with a bounce in her step and Kara humming along beside her.

"Kara, do you think Adam and I look good together?"

"Yes, sure."

"I don't know. He's much taller than me. I don't want to be one of those couples people say are mismatched."

"If he's the right guy, I don't see what difference it makes what other people think."

Viv chattered on while Kara's thoughts turned to how wonderful it felt to be with Nate. *Too bad he was a scuba diver and had such a dangerous job.*

But she wouldn't think of his dangerous job tonight. She'd enjoy the evening.

The deep red halter dress Kara spotted in the shop window fit well. As she paid for her purchase, she realized she'd just bought a dress to match her nail polish. That was a first.

*A sexy, red dress.* So unlike her. More like Viv. No wonder Viv was smirking. *Well, this isn't about Viv. It feels good to treat myself.*

Kara pulled the red dress she'd wear to dinner on and looked in the mirror. After a moment of contemplation she wound her hair up in a French twist, leaving her back and neck bare.

Viv emerged from the bathroom wearing an orange slip dress. *Only Viv can carry off a crayon color like that.*

"You look like an exotic island girl."

"Let's hope Adam thinks so." Viv slid gold bangles onto her wrists that jangled as she moved. "I'm just glad you found someone so fast. I thought it would take much longer. But this is great! I don't have to spend time worried about finding you a guy. Now Adam and I can have fun without worrying over you."

*Why did she think I'd have trouble finding a guy? Is that how she thinks of me? Poor, sad, Kara, whose husband was shot in front of her and who can't get her own date? That's exactly what she thinks. And it's kind of insulting. I don't need her to "find me a guy". That's not why I came on this cruise.*

"Nobody needs to find me a guy." She frowned as she dug through her makeup bag looking for a lipstick to go with her new red dress. "Don't you worry about me." Disgusted that the colors were all wrong and she couldn't find what she wanted, she tossed the bag on the bed. "You and Adam go on and have fun."

Viv chattered on about Adam, but Kara tuned her out.

*We've had a nice day, hanging out doing girl things. But maybe we both need some alone time.*

It had been years since she and Viv had spent so much time together. Viv was starting to get on her nerves. Tonight, Kara vowed, she wouldn't let Viv dominate the conversation. She'd work at not being shy and tongue-tied.

But she couldn't allow Nate to feed her again. The memory of the simple act still hovered. She'd enjoy it if they were alone, though. But not with the others there. What she needed was...

How many years since she'd been intimate with a man? A small shipboard romance would be okay. She could hardly wait to see Nate again.

Viv primped in the mirror, fussing with her hair.

*How long does it take her to get ready? She'll make us late to dinner if she keeps this up. Her hair doesn't look any different than it did thirty minutes ago when she should've been ready.*

*Why is Viv so obsessed with how she looks? Shouldn't she have outgrown that in high school? If anything it's gotten worse. Takes her twice as long to get ready as it used to. And she never bothered to say thank you for the pedicure I just used my certificate to buy for her. Would it kill her to say thank you?*

"Can you hurry up?" Kara paced as she waited.

Viv halted, hair spray bottle in hand and raised one eyebrow. "Oh, you did not just tell me to hurry up." She picked up her room card key and spun on her heel. "Let's go."

Viv did the marching step down the hall that she always did when she was pissed off, fast as her short stride would go, Kara following along behind, her longer legs having no trouble keeping up.

Kara was relieved to see Nate and Adam waiting for them at the table.

"Good evening, ladies," Nate said with a nod and a slow perusal of appreciation.

"Good evening." Kara slid into her seat with a smile only for Nate, enjoying the way he looked at her and noting how Viv bristled because neither man paid her any attention.

*Was Viv jealous? How much different she behaves now that I'm single again and ready to date.*

It was at that moment she realized she truly was

ready to date. Nate made it seem easy, less intimidating. Why had she been so nervous about dating?

She sat up in her chair, leaned toward Nate and said, "Please pass the rolls."

"Certainly." He reached for the silver basket and handed it to her, their fingers brushing as their eyes met. "Butter?"

"Yes, please."

Even the most mundane exchange between them held an almost electric charge. It was simply happening and she wasn't even trying.

Vernon and Phyllis, the elderly couple celebrating their anniversary, ordered a bottle of champagne for the table. They'd obviously made up, and the newlyweds had joined them for dinner tonight in honor of the older couple's anniversary.

Once everyone had a glass, Vernon raised his glass in a toast. "To my lovely wife and the happiest years of my life." He glanced around the table. "And to falling in love. May you fall hard and land softly into welcoming arms."

*Oh, God, yes. Welcoming arms. Oh, how I wish ... How I want that.*

"Hear, hear," William and Beverly, the newlyweds echoed.

The tinkle of glasses rang.

*They're lucky to have had so many years together.*

Kara blinked through misty eyes as she sipped champagne. Then Nate's warm, strong hand gave her knee a gentle squeeze before releasing it. She set her glass down and sent him a smile. He'd made her feel better with that squeeze as if he'd known she was a little choked up.

The waiter moved to take her order. The menu was a blur through watery eyes, so she ordered the waiters recommendations.

Kara waited for Nate to order before she started a conversation. But once again Viv beat her to it.

"What's your guilty food pleasure?" Viv asked leaning toward Nate.

Kara arched her eyebrows.

*What does she think she is doing? Same old Viv, insisting the spotlight be planted firmly on her.*

"Mine is Godiva chocolate," Viv purred.

"Pecan pie," Adam said recapturing Viv's attention.

Kara wondered what annoyed Viv more, the men paying attention to Kara or the fact Kara forced Viv to shorten her beauty routine.

"My favorite is tiramisu," Kara jumped into the conversation and gave her whole attention to Nate, ignoring Viv. "It's the one desert I can never pass up, even when I'm full."

"I love tiramisu," Nate said and the smile he sent her warmed her to her toes.

"Is that your guilty food pleasure too?" Kara asked.

He leaned in close to Kara and said in a low

voice, "My guilty pleasure is whipped cream on naked skin."

"Oh my." Her eyes widened and the thought of him licking whipped cream off her skin sent tingles down her back. She'd never experienced that. Nate could turn the simplest thing into the most sensual, and he did it in such a playful way. Images of what he'd described now filled her head, making her squirm in her seat as he watched her with mischievous eyes. His gaze deepened as she squirmed.

"Tonight's show is 'In the Mood.' It's love songs from Broadway shows," Viv gushed. "I love musicals and theater."

"How about you?" Nate asked Kara.

*Whipped cream or ... oh no, wait. Theater. He means what do I think about theater. Or does he?*

"Viv loves drama. Me, I'm more into old movies."

"You're more of a cuddle up at home to watch movies kind of girl?"

"Well, yes. Though I like going out to see movies and sometimes theater."

"I enjoy watching old movies too."

*One more thing we have in common.*

"And cuddling."

*Oh how good it would feel to cuddle up with him, sharing a bowl of popcorn.*

"Mmm, that sounds wonderful." Images of cuddling up next to him filled her head as she directed her attention back to her food, beneath his gaze and warm smile.

Though she may have forgotten how to date, being with Nate was easy. After dinner, the four of them sat together at the show, Nate on one side of Kara and Viv on the other. Viv turned sideways, all her attention on Adam, ignoring Kara.

The glittering costumes and musical numbers dazzled with sequined gowns, lights and great singing. The show would have captured Kara's attention entirely if not for the way Nate's fingers traced the back of her hand.

The touch of his fingers sent tingles all through her body, and the hum, which never faded when he was near, built within her. Thoughts of how they'd dance later and the hope he might kiss her again filled her mind.

Though he didn't look at her, she sensed he paid attention to her reaction, her slightest breath.

After the show, Viv said, "We'll freshen up and meet you guys in the nightclub in thirty minutes."

"We'll be waiting," Adam replied.

"Hurry back." Nate held her hand as Kara looked up into his eyes.

"I will."

Thirty minutes seemed like forever but at least Viv didn't dawdle in front of the mirror this time. She also didn't speak to Kara.

A quick brush of her teeth and a dash of lip-gloss and Kara was ready.

Viv dropped her lipstick into her bag. "I'm ready."

"Let's go."

Heading to the club, Viv walked like a racehorse itching to break stride. The deck was slick, and Kara slid into a bench. "Ouch."

Viv stopped. "You okay?"

Kara rubbed her thigh as the muscle throbbed. "Yes."

"Dancing will make you forget about it." Viv tapped a toe, impatient.

"I'm fine. Let's go."

Kara's thigh hurt and was going to bruise. Fair skinned, she bruised easy. The anticipatory hum that had built within had fled when she ran into the bench. She couldn't wait to see Nate.

As they entered the nightclub, pulsing neon lights underneath the dance floor lit the dim room. A DJ called out the next tune with a dedication. Kara followed Viv to the bar. They perched on stools and scanned the room for Adam and Nate, who soon appeared beside them after making their way through the crowded club.

A slow song started. Nate stood and held out his hand. "If you're ready, I'll claim that dance now."

Kara's heart gave a leap. Her stomach fluttered before she placed her hand in his. Warm, strong fingers closed over hers and he led her to the dance floor, maneuvering through the crowd with ease. He turned, smiled, and pulled her close.

The minute he took her in his arms everything around them faded away from her mind. He slid his left hand around her waist and twined the fingers of his right hand through hers. She placed her hand on his shoulder. How strong and solid he was beneath her fingertips. He held her with a strong, firm grasp.

He swung her around and she caught her breath. The warmth of his hand through the waist of the silk dress heated her skin as he pulled her closer, his eyes darkening as they gazed down into hers.

"Silky smooth," he said, the corners of his eyes turning up as he smiled.

Her heart hammered against her ribs. They moved in time to the music, around and around. Nick's dark lashes framed deep brown eyes that smoldered as he watched her.

She could stay in his arms and never return home again.

She was falling.

*No.*

She couldn't fall. *Not for one night or one week.*

*It would be so easy to fall in love with him.*

She couldn't bear it.

*Love meant loss and a broken heart. Again.*

# CHAPTER SEVEN

ate pulled Kara closer, and his hands moved down to her waist where he held her light as if she were made of glass. Her shyness made him move slow, though he wanted nothing more than to carry her off and make passionate love to her. She was everything his dream woman would be. Soft feminine curves and long silky hair enticing him to touch, sweet voice and loving eyes. Beyond the physical though, which called to him so strong, there was something else, something deep and primal that had no name.

The silk dress slid beneath his fingers, the only thing between them, and he felt the curve of her hip, the way she moved under his touch, letting him know the way she might move beneath him in a different kind of dance.

Her eyes glanced at him and away before

glancing back, which deepened his smile. He knew the subtle signs a woman sent, even unaware, in the dance of courtship.

She felt good in his arms. Her scent intoxicated him.

The nightclub thinned out. Nate swung Kara into a corner. Her steps faltered. His hands settled firm upon her hips to guide her. He kissed her just below the ear, blew soft in her ear, and then pulled away, holding her just enough at a distance to look down into her eyes.

His eyes searched hers. The green eyes gazing back at him held desire, excitement, a touch of nervousness, and a deep hunger.

"I'd like to go up on deck and see the stars." She spoke in a soft voice.

"All right, sweetheart." Threading his fingers through hers he led her across the room to the door.

He opened the door for her and then joined her, sliding his arm around her waist, pulling her close. "It will be windy." He glanced at the silk dress she wore. "Might be chilly."

He placed a soft kiss upon her temple and noted how warm her skin was. Perhaps either overheated from the dance floor or perhaps something else. Even though the ship had moved into warmer waters, nights at sea could be cool even in the Caribbean. They wouldn't stay out long or she might catch a chill.

They stepped outside and walked to the top deck as the breeze picked up, blowing her dress against her form. At the rails he pulled her close and rubbed her arms up and down. "Don't want you to catch a chill."

"Let's go down one level, out of the wind."

"Yes, good idea. It's cooler out than I thought."

They moved down the steps and over by the lounge chairs. He reversed one around so it faced the ocean instead of the pool. "We can relax and watch the ocean for a while. I'll hold you and keep you warm."

Women always sought his warmth. They'd snuggle in bed, seeking heat, wanting to be held. He enjoyed warming them, holding them close. One lover had even said he heated her from the inside out. He was used to women seeking his heat.

But Kara sought nothing from him.

*It was refreshing. There was something special about her.*

He didn't want to lose her. The more he spent time with Kara, the more time he wanted to spend with her.

They sat together, her back against his chest, his arms around her while bright stars shone overhead and the ocean moved in dark silence. He leaned his cheek against her head.

"I like holding you."

He felt her smile, along with her sigh.

"I like it too."

She nestled in closer, rubbing against him, and he tightened his arms around her.

KARA WATCHED the white caps in the ocean, enjoying the feel of Nate's arms around her, the warmth and strength in his body, his warm, spicy scent and the rumble in his chest as he murmured in her ear, his voice sending tingles down her neck.

She hadn't been held this way for a long time. Perhaps never held exactly this way. Kara closed her eyes to listen to Nate's voice, the quiet sounds of the ocean and the wind; the rapid beat of her heart.

She wished they could stay like this forever.

*It was an impossible wish. He would get off the ship and go back to his job. She might never see him again.*

She tried not to trust in wishes. She'd let the evening take her where it would. She didn't want to live with regret.

When he began kissing her ear, she gave herself up into the feeling, losing track of time as if nothing existed but this moment.

Nate tensed and she wondered what was wrong.

A drunken man almost fell into their deck chair.

"Hey, you know a good party? All the nightclubs are closed. Won't give me another drink."

Nate lifted Kara off of his lap and stood in front of her as he faced the man. "No, we don't."

The man tried to look around behind Nate, but he shifted his body sideways, blocking the man's view of Kara.

"What you got back there? Anything to drink?"

"No." Nate took Kara by the hand. They moved past the man.

"Where you goin'?"

"Come on, sweetheart, I'll walk you to your cabin," Nate said.

Kara wondered if Viv would be in the cabin. She'd ignored Kara all evening as she hung onto Adam.

Nate walked Kara to her cabin then leaned one hand against the wall. "I had a wonderful evening."

"Me too."

His lips met hers in a soft kiss. Her heart fluttered. It was a deep, delicious kiss.

They came up for air and she caught her breath. She turned and fumbled with the card key. "Would you like to come in?"

"Yes, I'd like that very much." His hand closed over hers, calming her nerves. "Here, sweetheart. Let me." He pulled open the door as she walked in, then followed behind her, pulling the door closed.

*Good. Viv is gone. Now is not the time to be shy.*

She placed the key on the table and turned to him, placing her hands on his chest. "Kiss me again."

His eyes flared and he smiled. He bent toward her. Her eyes closed as his lips touched hers.

The kiss was sweet, tender. Her lips parted and it deepened, his tongue danced with hers. He kissed her lips, her cheek, and across to her ear, tickling her with his tongue, raining kisses down her neck.

Giving her a lazy smile, which said they had all night, he sat on the bed, taking her by the hands and pulling her closer.

The silk slid across her skin as she moved.

His warm fingers moved over her hips, pulling her dress up, finding the outline of her lacy, bikini panties. His fingers traced her skin in a slow pattern, teasing her, warming her. He moved so slowly she wanted to cry out.

*Oh yes, please touch me.*

But then his hands moved away and the silk fell down across her hips again.

"Your roommate is here."

Viv slid the key in the lock.

"Oh, no." Disappointment filled her as Nate stood.

Viv opened the door.

"Good night, sweetheart, I had a wonderful evening," Nate said.

"Me too."

Viv stood with a look of surprise on her face.

"Give me a good night kiss before I go?" Nate asked.

Kara smiled and nodded.

He gave her a sweet, soft kiss. "Sleep well, sweetheart. I'll see you tomorrow."

"Yes, see you tomorrow."

He turned. "Good evening Viv."

"Evenin'." Viv stepped aside to let him pass. She closed the door, came in, and plopped on her bed. "Was I interrupting?" She smirked.

Disappointed in the lost moment and not wanting Viv to see that, Kara turned her back and pulled off the dress then reached for her nightgown. "We were just saying good night." She didn't want to discuss Nate with Viv right now. She wanted to linger in the memory of his kisses.

"Girl, if Nate is anything like his cousin you're in for a treat. Why aren't you giving it up to that hunky man?" Viv smirked again.

"Stop it, Viv." Kara slipped into the nightgown and turned back around.

"You need to loosen up. Give him the green light." Viv wiggled her eyebrows. "Then leave the rest up to Nate. It's been a long time for you, but he knows what to do."

*And what is the green light? No, I'm not even going to ask.*

"Oh, for God's sake. I was married. I know what to do."

"But you're rusty." Viv leaned forward onto her

elbows. She cupped her head in her hands and rushed on. "I'll give you pointers."

Kara crossed her arms. They were not still in high school and this was hardly her first date, even if it had been many years.

"I don't need pointers."

"You intrigue Nate. He must find you mysterious. Since you haven't given it up, you're still a challenge."

Kara, shocked by the way Viv continued to speak to her on this cruise, frowned. *When did Viv become so careless with our friendship that she thinks she can speak to me that way? When had this started?*

*Ever since we boarded this ship she hasn't been the same Viv I used to know.* Kara was not in agreement with Viv's theories on dating. Viv's smug expression irritated Kara so much she wanted to change the subject.

"You ran off with Adam quick enough. What about Rory?"

"Rory and I aren't exclusive and he's back in Britain. You're changing the subject." Viv smirked. "What you need is to get laid."

"I do not need to get laid."

*Maybe you need to get laid. You're the one being bitchy.*

"Liar."

Kara bunched up her pillow and threw it at Viv. "Stop it, Viv. I don't need your help."

Viv threw it back at her. "Then live a little."

Kara squeezed the pillow in both hands. Viv made her want to scream. "I am living."

"Bloody hell. You're not living. You're just going through the motions."

"You don't understand anything."

Viv's face turned red and she exploded. "No, I don't. I never had a husband to lose, which you've rubbed my nose in. Get knotted!" Viv ran into the bathroom, slamming the door.

*What the hell was that all about? ... If I have to hear one more of Viv's little British expressions, I'll jump overboard. I really will.*

Kara wanted to scream in frustration.

Viv burst out of the bathroom again. "You think I don't have feelings? You made Neil your whole life and shut me out. I know what Neil used to say about me. *Poor Viv can't keep a man. Goes through a new one every month.* You think that doesn't hurt? But let me tell you something. *I'm* living *my* life. Neil is dead. And you might as well be. You're wasting your life mooning over a man you think was perfect. He wasn't. He came on to me, Kara. You don't know how he really was."

*What?* Tears stung Kara's eyes. *How dare she talk about Neil that way? ... What if it was true?*

"Neil was a good man." Kara choked as tears overcame her. "He wouldn't have."

*Why didn't she tell me this before? Why now? He wouldn't have. Viv was my best friend. So how could she? What kind of friend is she? Why is she acting like this?*

All the frustration she'd held inside turned loose and she curled up, sobbing into the pillow.

Viv rushed to her side and put her arm around Kara. "Hey, I'm sorry. I didn't mean to hurt you." She bowed her head to touch Kara's forehead. "It's okay. Don't cry. I know you still miss him. I'm sorry for what I said. I wasn't ever gonna tell."

Kara nodded and took a deep rattling breath to calm herself. "Viv, I never meant to shut you out."

Viv reached for a tissue. "We both went off the deep end." She handed it to Kara. "It's been a long evening, it's late, and we're both tired. I won't bring it up again. But I'm glad you know. Glad it's out." She sat back and her eyes lit up. "Tell you what. Tomorrow you choose what you want to do. I'll follow along quiet as a mouse." She raised one hand. "I promise."

Kara used the tissue to wipe her tears but the realization her best friend was not the friend she used to be still hurt. Just when she'd gotten over losing Neil, it was another blow.

Viv waited for her to speak.

"No, Viv. I need some time alone. Tomorrow I just want to do my own thing."

"Oh. Well, if that's what you want."

They prepared for bed, stepping around each other. Kara fell into bed as exhaustion claimed her

When Viv turned out the light Kara exhaled a sigh of relief.

She lay in bed thinking, unable to fall asleep. *Is Viv right?* Was Neil not the man she'd thought he was? Kara glanced over at Viv, who was now snoring. *She can sleep now her conscience is clear. Great. But she's thrown this at me just before bedtime. And she knows I have trouble sleeping.*

Kara wasn't sure what shocked her more: the way her best friend was behaving or the accusation. Which might not even be true. Viv tended to exaggerate things when she wanted more attention.

Finally Kara dozed off but then the dream came again.

She was with Neil at the Washington Zoo. Animals moved about in the cool air of early fall and leaves fluttered down as Neil held her hand. They passed a panther pacing the worn path in his enclosure and found the Great Ape House. Neil mimicked the gorilla that watched him with black eyes as he scratched his stomach with human like fingers.

"I wonder what he's thinking?" Kara said.

"He's thinking me want food." Neil scratched his stomach. "Me want hot dog. Me want to kiss pretty lady."

She laughed. He brought her near for a kiss. When a little boy behind them said, "Eeww," they broke apart laughing.

They ate chili dogs on the way to see the pandas. The sun's rays warmed Kara. It was a perfect day.

At the panda enclosure the pandas were eating. She'd thought giant pandas would be big, but these were cute little cubs with black ears and black ringed eyes. They rolled back as if in recliners, their paws and claws grasping pieces of bamboo twice the length of their bodies. It was a special moment for Kara. She had always wanted to see the pandas.

Neil's phone rang and he answered. "Can't talk. I'm at the zoo, remember? Call you later."

The call brought on that hushed urgency in his tone. Then Neil asked her to wait by the entrance to the zoo while he went into the gift shop. He came out holding a soft, black and white, stuffed panda, and she laughed and gave him a big hug and a kiss to thank him. He asked the gray-haired man nearby to take their picture. He handed the man his camera, pulled her close, and they both smiled for the photo.

On the way home, they stopped for gas. Neil got out to fill up the car.

A shot rang out.

Neil crumpled to the ground.

Kara woke gasping. She tried the breathing exercises to stop the panic. She was safe in the ship's cabin, not the car. She hadn't had the dream in months. She'd forgotten about the phone call. Now her thoughts raced.

*Who had called Neil?*

She might never know.

*It was Sunday. His day off.* There'd been calls on his cell phone at odd times during that trip. She'd never know what those phone calls had been about, but he was a contractor and calls came in at odd hours. It went with the job.

But he was gone now. She couldn't confront him. What should she do with this? Why did Viv tell her now?

She got up for a glass of water and noticed a package on the desk next to the vase of flowers. A box of Godiva chocolates and an envelope with her name on it. Had Nate sent them? Their kissing kept them too busy to notice it was there. Maybe he had. She opened the envelope.

# CHAPTER EIGHT

*S*weets *for the sweetest girl in the world. Daryl.*
Her heart sank.

*They weren't from Nate. Had Daryl sent the flowers too?*

It was nice to receive gifts, but this ... First the expensive spa certificate and now this. Why was Daryl sending gifts? He was her boss and a bon voyage gift was thoughtful, but he'd sent more than one and he'd been acting strange before she left too. As if he didn't really want her to go, though from everything he'd said he was all for it.

Viv was acting strange. Daryl was acting strange. *Nothing was strange before I won this cruise and now it's like everything in my world has shifted somehow.*

She glanced at Viv, who rolled over and snored. Kara opened the desk drawer and shoved the chocolates in. *If Viv doesn't see them I won't have to explain.*

She got back into bed, but tossed and turned.

*If it was true that Neil propositioned Viv, there must have been others.* Her mind shifted, sorting facts but giving her no answers.

Neil had always said they had a perfect marriage. Kara had learned not to want too much. That way he couldn't disappoint her.

As she lay in the dark, her inner voice told her she wanted the magic. Wanted to be loved, treasured, and cared for. Wanted a full life, not the one she'd been living.

Viv snorted in her sleep and rolled over.

*This cruise has not turned out anything like I'd hoped.*

Kara watched the newsletter with the day's events slide under the door as someone did each morning.

*It's time I took a day to myself.*

The note she left for Viv said, "Taking some me time." Kara showered, dressed and left.

Kara stopped in the Parisian pastry café to load up on caffeine since she hadn't slept. Then she went to watch the culinary art demonstration where chefs prepared food and carved fruits and vegetables into sculptures, followed by the art of napkin folding and a galley tour.

She went to the open house bridge visit to meet the captain and see how the ship was steered, and took a Texas Two Step lesson. Though she stayed busy, thoughts of Nate crept in. Before each event she scanned the room for him and wondered what he was doing, but the entire day passed without a glimpse.

How could she miss him so much when they'd only just met?

Kara reached the dining room early, having managed to avoid Viv by getting ready for dinner early. She'd already ordered when Nate and Adam arrived with Viv.

"I missed you today." Nate sat beside her.

His husky voice sent a ripple of awareness through her. Somehow her feelings for him had intensified.

"I went on the tours to see the bridge and the galley and watch the chefs. Then took a country line dance class."

His eyes lit. "Practicing your moves?" He winked. "You can show me tonight."

"It was line dancing," Viv said with a dismissive shrug.

Nate raised one eyebrow at Viv and directed his attention to Kara. "I'll uh, look forward to seeing what you've learned."

"Tonight's theme is country western," Kara said. "I'm looking forward to it."

"Adam and I have plans this evening. You're on your own, Kara," Viv said.

"Have fun."

*I'm sure I'll have a much better time without you.*

"I'd be happy to take you dancing tonight, or anywhere else you'd care to go," Nate said with a smile, his brown eyes like warm chocolate.

Just like the chocolate she could never stay away from, his eyes kept drawing her gaze back to him.

"I'd hoped to see you today," Nate said. "But I'm glad you had fun."

She smiled. "What did you do today?"

"Spent my day hoping to catch a glimpse of a beautiful siren I met the other night." Nate watched Kara, smiling when she blushed.

When her food came out she looked at the green noodles in surprise. She didn't remember ordering green noodles. Nate distracted her, kept her off balance.

She ate a small bite, but realized she had lost her appetite. Something about the green just put her off.

Nate gestured to her plate, "Order something else if you don't like it."

"Oh no, it's fine. I'm just not as hungry as I thought."

Their waiter bent near Kara. "Madame, would you like me to bring you something else?"

"No, really, I'm fine." She gestured for him to take her plate away. "I'll wait for desert."

The waiter took her plate and she nibbled on her roll. She moved her hand from her lap to her stomach hoping to calm the slight queasiness. Nate's gaze caught the movement. She moved her hand back to her lap and gave him a small smile.

Desert arrived. Angel food cake, fruit, and whipped crème.

"Trifle." Nate picked up his fork. "Should be delicious." He lifted the bite on his fork to her lips. "Try some trifle."

"Are you trifling with me?" she teased in a low tone, the image of him tempting her with the sweet dessert making it impossible for her to say no as a smile crept across her face.

"Only if you want me to, sweetheart."

She laughed and opened her mouth. He slid the fork in. Her lips closed over it and he slid it out. The way he looked at Kara made her want to curl her toes. She sat with her lips pursed and her mouth full of sweet trifle. Suddenly she couldn't swallow.

*He's feeding me again. Why does this feel sensual and naughty?*

"Is something wrong? Don't you like it?" A mischievous gleam entered his eyes.

Oh, he was trifling with her. *He knew exactly what was wrong.* The look in his eyes said he enjoyed every minute.

*The last time he fed me it was salty as the sea. Tonight he's being sweet.*

She swallowed so she could answer him.

"It's quite good." He took a bite, leaving a rim of whipped cream on his lip.

"Yes," she murmured, watching as his tongue slid out to lick the whipped cream off.

She swallowed again hard as she watched his tongue, remembering what he'd said earlier about whipped cream on heated skin and thinking how his tongue would feel against her skin. The thought made her feel warm and melty inside.

Her mouth suddenly dry, she took a drink of water to cool down and clear her head.

"The raspberry trifle is delicious," she said.

"Whipped cream is delicious." Nate's deep brown eyes crinkled at the corners as he grinned. "You uh, did ask what my guilty pleasure was."

*Oh my. He's not just talking about this dessert.*

She blushed again. She took another drink of water hoping to cool the heat in her cheeks.

"Kara, I'd like to take you on the Rhino Rider excursion tomorrow," Nate said.

"What's that?"

"Adam and I are going," Viv interrupted. "I can't wait."

"We'll ride a Rhino Rider out to a cove to snorkel," Nate said. "You'll love it. Trust me. You'll be in good hands."

Kara relaxed her shoulders. A boat ride sounded like fun. She pictured them riding along on one of those glass-bottomed boats, watching the fish and feeling the slow breeze. She wasn't sure about snorkeling. If she didn't feel up to trying, she could always watch from the boat.

"All right." Kara smiled. "That does sound like fun."

"Good." Nate smiled back. "It will be."

After dinner Nate and Kara strolled past the bars, listening to the different styles of music. The piano bar was playing classical music and in one of the show lounges there was big band music. Country music played at the main dance club were they headed.

They stepped inside and he pulled her closer, raising his voice over the music. "You ready to teach me?"

"The dances I learned were line dances. Not couple dances." Disappointment threaded through her. She wanted him to touch her.

"That's just fine, sweetheart. You can teach me those first, then we'll slow dance."

They moved onto the dance floor, and Nate lined up next to Kara. She looked up into his eyes. "It's really easy," she said. "Just stand by me and follow my moves."

He smiled down at her. "Stand by you? You bet."

A song started, and the dancers began to move. Step, slide, step, slide, turn step again. Nate's legs moved in a slow easy athletic slide to the music as he watched her.

Halfway through the song, Kara noticed he

picked up the moves quickly and barely watched her feet. His gaze stayed upon her face, yet he didn't miss step.

*He already knows the steps.*

When they stopped and found a table, Kara asked. "Have you done these dances before?"

A slow grin spread across his face. "Well, yes. My dad's side of the family is from Texas."

Kara frowned in confusion. "But you wanted me to teach you. Why if you already knew how?"

"I couldn't help myself." He grinned deeper. "The thought of you teaching me was enticing."

"But that's silly."

*Why would he want me to teach him something he already knew? Didn't most men like telling women how to do things?*

"Call me silly," his brow arched up, and he leaned forward, placing his finger beneath her chin. "You can teach me whatever you like."

His words delighted her mind as his touch ignited her body.

She swallowed hard. "I like to slow dance best."

His eyes searched hers. "Then we'll dance really slowly."

She smiled and he released her chin.

THE SUN WAS JUST RISING as Nate climbed the steps to the top deck. Kara stood by the rail watching the ship pull into the dock at St. Martin. Viv yawned at her side.

Happy to see Kara, he was less pleased to see her roommate. Last night the woman had interrupted them once again in Kara's room, just as they'd begun making out.

It was as if he was back in high school with a girl-friend he could never be alone with for anything beyond a kiss. Which would have been slightly less irritating if the woman treated Kara better. He didn't care for the way Viv treated her and wondered why Kara put up with it.

"It's a clear morning," Nate said as he approached them.

Kara turned to reply, her fair hair blown into disarray by the wind. Her eyes met his and reflected the same startling blue as the sky behind her. She took his breath away.

"Smashing," Viv said. "Kara was madly keen on getting up early to see this." Viv's tone said she'd rather not be up.

"I've never seen a ship this size dock before. I, I didn't want to miss it." Kara looked down at men uncoiling the large ropes before letting them down to where other men fastened them to the pier. The narrow pier stuck out some distance from the shops.

A handful of people stood below watching from the pier.

Kara glanced down at a man who paced below. She frowned. "Something about him seems familiar."

"Oh my God," Viv said. "I don't believe it." She turned to Kara. "Is that Daryl?"

Shock crossed Kara's face. "No, it can't be. It must be someone who looks like him."

*Obviously Daryl was bad news. Any man who could cause that look on Kara's face ought to be shot.*

Her hands clenched the rail as she looked down at the man.

*Who is he? And why is Kara reacting this way?*

Nate looked from Kara to Viv and waited but neither of the women attempted to explain.

He looked down at the man. "Who is he? Ex boyfriend?"

"He's just a friend." Kara bristled. "From work."

*Her friend from work was anxious to catch her attention.*

Nate raised an eyebrow.

"He's her boss." Viv said. "Her very demanding boss."

"Demanding?"

"He wanted to come on this trip with her. Can you believe that? Cheeky bloke."

"Viv, what he said was if you couldn't go he'd take your place."

Nate gazed at Kara and it struck him how naïve she was. He watched her, remembering she'd told him she married young.

"I'll just bet he would," Viv said.

"It isn't like that," Kara shook her head. "He's just a friend. And he's my boss. I'm not going on vacation with him."

"Sure looks like he's determined to go on yours." Viv snorted and shook her head.

"Security won't let him on board," Nate slipped an arm around Kara, who had a bewildered expression on her face.

Daryl's red face and the way his hands were gesturing indicated he was having a heated discussion below with the security guards. Then he looked up and shouted, "Kara," waving one arm.

She frowned slightly and raised her hand instead of waving.

"Guess I'll have to go see what he wants." Kara sighed.

"I knew you were gonna say that," Viv crossed her arms.

"Do you want me to tag along?" Nate asked.

"No, it's no big deal. Really." Kara squared her shoulders and walked toward the stairs.

He had a bad feeling about this guy and when he got a bad feeling, it was always right.

Viv shot him a look. "Daryl calls her way more than a boss should."

"Is it work related?"

"Stupid stuff. Any excuse to call her."

"Sounds like he has a crush on Kara."

"He does. But why the hell is he here? This is supposed to be *her* vacation." Viv frowned. "I don't like it."

*That's one thing we agree on.*

Nate nodded. "Thanks for giving me a heads up."

"Yeah. Well, see you on the dock. Looking forward to the excursion. I'd better catch up with her now."

"Yes. See you on the pier."

*Good. Viv would look after Kara. She won't be alone with that guy.*

Nate turned to look back down at Daryl and frowned. It was good Viv was going with her. His gut told him Daryl showing up on the island wasn't a good situation.

# CHAPTER NINE

$\mathcal{K}$ara barely reached the bottom of the gangplank before Daryl leaned forward waving. "Kara!"

The uniformed guard standing on the pier just below the gangplank held out his hand and said, "Step back, sir."

Kara forced a smile. "Hello, Daryl. What a surprise."

"Hello, gorgeous. Look at you! The cruise is agreeing with you. But you can tell me all about it soon. I have a surprise for you. Go change. I'm taking you to brunch now, and then we'll tour around the island. Make a day of it."

"No can do," Viv who'd hurried to catch up with Kara, interrupted before Kara could reply. "We're signed up for a Rhino Rider Boat Tour at twelve thirty."

"So cancel it."

"It's too late for refunds," Viv said.

He frowned, his dislike for Viv evident. "I'll reimburse you both."

"You can't. We didn't pay for it, someone else did." Viv smirked.

He scowled deeper. "Who?"

"It doesn't matter. It's what we're going to do today."

"Okay," Kara said, wishing they wouldn't fight. "I'll go to brunch as long as I'm back in time for the boat tour."

Viv rolled her eyes. "Whatever, Kara. Just be back in time."

"I will be."

"Go change. I'll wait here for you." Daryl gestured to the guard. "They won't let me board."

"They don't let anyone on board without a room card," Kara said. "It's not just you." She looked down at her shorts and T-shirt. Her tee shirt had a palm tree and monkeys on it. Daryl was wearing a shirt, tie, and dress slacks.

"Hurry up," he said, "We have reservations."

If she'd been wearing something other than this silly tee shirt, she'd go as she was. But she could see he wouldn't want to go somewhere nice with her wearing this.

"All right."

"If you're going to change, I'll go back with you and find Adam," Viv said.

"Okay." Kara waved at Daryl, who was now on his cell phone, scowling. She walked with Viv back up the gangplank.

Once they reached the room, Viv went to spin the dial on the room safe. "Take your watch and keep an eye on the time. And keep your cell phone on. I'll take mine. I, I don't trust him to get you back here before we leave."

"Maybe you don't, but I doubt he'd deliberately make me miss our excursion."

"If I were you, I'd make sure I had enough cab fare to get back. He'll conveniently forget the time."

"I'll be there on time."

"You'd better be." Viv called Adam. "Hey, glad I caught ya. There's been a small change in plans."

Kara jerked the closet door open. It hit the wall with a thud.

*Okay, settle down. It's just brunch. I'll go, thank him, and then meet up with Viv and the guys. Daryl and I go to lunch all the time. It's no big deal to have lunch with him.*

Her stomach twisted.

*That's different from him showing up on my vacation. Oh my God. Can I not even go on vacation without work following? I need a new job. Have to create a resume. The minute I get back. Why is he here? It must* be a last minute trip. He didn't say anything about it before.

He'd said he wanted to see St. Martin. Getting a last minute ticket to the island must have cost dearly. Or was this trip business?

And what made him think she'd drop her plans because he showed up and wanted to do something?

Her stomach flipped again.

In case she was late, Kara left her red bikini on and pulled a cotton sundress over it. She put on her watch, and grabbed her wallet. She rolled up one of the beach towels the cruise line provided to use while ashore and put it in her bag. If she had to, she'd go straight from brunch to the pier to catch the boat.

*What will Nate think of me going off with Daryl?*

On the way down in the elevator, Kara turned on her phone. Her stomach flipped again. Thirteen phone calls from Daryl. Text after text. She deleted everything. Whatever he wanted, he'd tell her at brunch.

*If it's work related, I don't really want to hear about work on my vacation. My God, can I not get a break? And if it isn't work related, well, that would be too weird. It has been nice to get a break from him. Being away from the phone is so freeing. Why can't he leave me alone when I'm on vacation?*

Daryl stood waiting with a smile. Kara tried to relax and smile back.

*There has to be a logical reason for him being here on the island. Daryl isn't the sort to do things on a whim.*

"You look very pretty, Kara."

"Thank you. How did you get here?"

"I flew. Tiny plane. Bumpy ride."

*That had to be expensive.*

"It was worth it."

Had she spoken out loud or had he read her mind?

"I'm glad you made time for me. I wanted to surprise you." He reached for her hand.

"Well, you certainly did." She pulled her hand loose. He was her boss. They didn't hold hands. Her stomach twisted again.

Kara wanted brunch over with so she could escape and go snorkeling with Nate. She wished Nate was here now and had wished for him by her side ever since walking away with Daryl.

But wishing didn't work. Because here she sat across the table from Daryl feeling decidedly uncomfortable. Nate was probably having fun and thinking about the excursion he seemed so excited to take her on. She just had to get past this brunch and then she'd be on the boat with Nate.

"I had breakfast on the ship. I'm not really hungry." She ordered the small fresh fruit plate to have something to nibble.

"Bring her the quiche and fruit combo," Daryl told the waiter.

"Oh no, that's too much food."

He ignored her and shooed the waiter away.

"If you insist on going on that crazy excursion, you need to do more than nibble on fruit."

"It's not crazy."

*God, he was pushy.*

They weren't at work now. There was no reason to boss her around here. And he'd insisted on ordering champagne.

"Drink up."

She frowned but sipped from her glass.

*What a fiasco. I should have said, 'No Daryl, I can't go. I made other plans.' He took me off guard. This is what's crazy. He might be my boss and a work friend, but this is my vacation. He shouldn't be here.*

Daryl kept talking but hadn't gotten around to the reason he showed up on her vacation and she was tired of dancing around the subject and tired of answering questions about her cruise as he grilled her.

With the glass of champagne her courage amplified and she interrupted him. "Daryl, what brings you to the island on such short notice? Why are you here?"

He paused, his eyes searched hers. "Since you brought it up," he reached across the table to place his hand over hers. "You brought me here."

She froze.

*Oh my God. This is not happening. He's my boss.*

Daryl smiled. "We started out as friends, Kara. Many couples start out that way. When you left, I realized how much I missed you and I had to see you."

"So you flew here on a whim because you missed me?"

"Yes, and the ship's manifest is full. I couldn't obtain passage or I would be sailing with you tonight celebrating the New Year. But they won't let me."

The revelation stunned her. His hand pinned hers against the table as she sat frozen.

She spoke but didn't move, waiting for her words to sink in. "Daryl, we're just friends. That's all we can be."

"I know you've been in mourning since your husband died. So I've held back. But I couldn't wait any longer."

She pulled her hand out from beneath his and shook her head. "Daryl, no I can't."

He cut her off. "Don't tell me you can't. You're obviously going off on that excursion with some guy. Who is he?"

She regretted answering his previous questions about the cruise. She wasn't about to answer this one.

"That's none of your business."

His fist closed around his napkin, squeezing it. He took a deep inhale then let it out and spoke succinctly. "It is my business. You're going off with some strange man and God only knows what might happen. Who is he?"

"He's an ex-Marine, so I'm sure I'll be fine."

Daryl leaned back in his chair and gave her an incredulous look. "A Marine."

"Yes." Kara put her fork down.

His eyes narrowed. "You weren't dating before. Insisted you weren't ready for dating."

"That was before this cruise."

"You couldn't wait for me."

"This has nothing to do with you Daryl." The thought of being intimate with Daryl turned her stomach. "We work together."

He cut her off. "No one has to know. It will be our secret. I appreciate your dedication to the job, but if you were mine you wouldn't have to work unless it was what you wanted. Give me a chance, Kara."

"Daryl, I can't go out with you. We can only be friends."

"Do not give me that we can only be friends bull-shit." His face turned stony and he called for the check.

"I value your friendship, Daryl."

"You need to reconsider." His voice raised and diners at other tables looked over.

She didn't answer. She didn't have anything else to say.

"One night, Kara. Let me wine and dine you tonight, treat you well. Give me tonight. Celebrate the New Year with me. You won't regret it."

*Oh God. I shouldn't have come.*

She couldn't wait to be back on the ship away from him, where he couldn't follow.

"No, Daryl. I can't."

He paid the bill and they walked back to the pier in silence. He was in no hurry and didn't hail a taxi. He scowled when she glanced at her watch.

*Everything is awkward now. How can I work for this guy for even one more day?*

Viv stood on the pier, holding their tickets and a blue and white "Dream Boat" beach towel that matched the one in Kara's bag. She was talking to Adam.

The tour guide began collecting tickets and directing passengers into van.

"We have to go," Viv gestured to her to come on, her protective side showing.

*Oh thank you Viv.*

Viv had never liked Daryl and for once, Kara was glad of it. Viv's assertiveness helped Kara to feel more confident without all the guilt saying no to Daryl usually created.

"Thank you for brunch," Kara said. "I'll see you back at the office.

"We need to talk, Kara," Daryl gripped her arm. "When will you be back from your tour? Have dinner with me and we can talk."

Kara pulled her arm away. "I don't know what time we'll get back, and we'll be sailing at dinnertime."

"You in line?" Nate asked Daryl, stepping up beside Kara and towering over her.

*Where had he come from? He's so quiet I never heard him approach.* A sense of relief flooded over her.

Daryl refused to answer or step out of the way. "Kara, have dinner with me on the island tonight. I'll make it a New Year's Eve to remember. I've made excellent reservations at a fine restaurant. You can board the ship on the next island."

Kara shook her head again. "No."

"The lady said no. Now, unless you're going on this excursion get out of the way," Nate growled.

Daryl stepped aside but his eyes burned with dislike for Nate.

Viv and Adam had already stepped into the van, and the guide said, "Ticket please."

Kara felt flustered, wondering how she'd board when Viv had her ticket.

Nate reached to hand the attendant two tickets and she exhaled.

*It's okay. Nate is taking care of everything.*

"Come on, Kara," Nate's gentle voice urged her, his stance protective, ready for anything.

"Daryl, I have to go now."

Kara stepped into the van, and Nate followed her, leaving Daryl standing on the dock watching. The guide swung the door shut and the van started up.

With eight people in the van, it was snug and warm as Christmas Calypso music played. Viv and Adam sat in the very back seat, and Kara knew they'd be making out.

"Here, sweetheart." Nate put his arm across the back of the seat and she scooted close to him. His arm wrapped around her shoulder making her feel safe.

The van pulled away.

Kara couldn't relax with Daryl standing on the pier watching them, but soon she couldn't see him anymore and let out a breath she hadn't realized she'd been holding.

*Thank God that's over and Nate is here now.*

"I'm proud of you for standing up to your boss."

"Thank you." She leaned her head against him and exhaled even deeper.

He ran his fingers across her arm where a slight bruise began to form, and watched her. "Hurt?"

She glanced down to where Daryl had gripped her arm. "Not as much as it looks. I bruise easy."

"He had no business touching you. That's assault, Kara. You could file a complaint."

"I don't want to think about him now." She closed her eyes.

Nate kissed her forehead. "All right, sweetheart." He gathered her closer within his arms. "Relax now. It's over."

The van reached the pier on the French side of St. Martin, a pretty, Caribbean island with pastel painted houses, and they climbed out.

Kara raised her hand to shelter her eyes and looked for the glass bottom boat. All she saw were extra wide jet skis for tourists bobbing in the water.

*Where is the boat?*

Then she saw the sign, Rhino Riders with a picture of a couple racing through the wind on one.

*Oh no.*

"You uh might want to step out of your dress and shoes," Nate said. "Stow your things in your bag."

Viv and Adam had slipped on life jackets and were waiting, Viv with an impatient look on her face.

*They were going out into the ocean on those jet skis. Oh, my god. What if I fall off? The ocean is deep.*

Everyone waited, looking at her. Nate held out her life jacket. Already she felt shaky from the brunch with Daryl and now they were going out into the ocean on those little machines. She wasn't ready. But Nate waited patiently. She slipped off her shoes, pulled the dress over her head and put them in her bag. The guide took her bag and dropped it into a large footlocker then locked it.

Nate spoke to the guide in a low voice and slipped him a folded bill.

The guide gave Nate a broad smile. "No problem."

*What is he arranging? Was any man who he seemed to be?*

First Viv accuses her husband and now Daryl shows up acting strange. She'd only just met Nate. She hoped he didn't get them into trouble.

"Come here, sweetheart."

She moved over by him, and he helped her on with her life jacket then fastened it. Again she felt looked after, just the way he looked after her at the lifeboat drill. He climbed on to the machine, threw a leg over the seat, and turned and held out his hand for her.

Kara stepped cautiously near the edge of the pier. *Oh God.* Fear rumbled through her stomach. The Rhino Rider appeared nothing more than a jet ski with an inflatable raft. Nate waited.

"Climb on, sweetheart. I promised I'd take good care of you, remember?" He smiled reassuringly. "Trust me."

She smiled wanly and placed her hand in his. Taking her hand to steady her, Nate helped her onto the back of the machine, her legs straddling the seat behind him. Turning the key, he revved the engine and went out slow through the no-wake zone to where the others now waited. Kara's arms clung around his waist.

"Hold on," he said. He increased speed to follow their guide.

Kara leaned forward close against his back, holding tight as they zoomed past the beach out into the open ocean.

Neither spoke against the roar of wind and the engine. She burrowed her face against his back away from the wind, her fingers against the muscles of his abs digging in; her breasts against his back, her bikini top the only thing between their bodies.

They crashed across waves, the rumble of the machine beneath them. Each time the Rhino Rider landed down on the waves, it pressed her into his back, creating friction.

Kara held on tight, drawing on his strength to help her combat her fear. His muscles flexed and moved with the machine. She sensed his exhilaration and confidence and clung to him, closing her eyes. The mix of fear and excitement was almost too much. She hid her face against the wind, breathing in his scent, his aftershave, and the suntan lotion. Touching him, skin to skin, her body thrummed.

Suddenly they slowed. She opened her eyes.

A black rock jutted out from the middle of a cove, and they were headed for it. They stopped near the rock, engines idling, with everyone circled around the guide.

"Kill the engines," he said, and they did.

All was silent.

"Now remember, this is a protected coral reef." The guide glanced at Nate and nodded. "We don't usually bring tourists here, so here are the rules. Don't bring anything back with you and don't touch the coral."

*So that's why he slipped the guide money. Thank God, it wasn't something illegal. Or is it?*

Everyone put on flippers and goggles. Viv and Adam dove into the water, neither of them glancing at Kara.

Nate handed her the snorkel gear then he sat on the edge of the boat, watching her as he put on his gear. "Need help, sweetheart?"

"I think I can do it."

"Make sure you get a good seal on your goggles. They need to be tight."

"Oh." She sat with her flippers on, feeling ridiculous. They were so big, sticking up over the edge of the Rhino Rider. She felt like a big, awkward duck.

The water loomed, deep and wide below her. Gulping back her fear, she wondered how she'd get in without a ladder. She was too afraid of water to dive or jump in. Either way she'd go under. Though she wore a life jacket today, she'd never been in a body of water larger than a swimming pool.

Nate pointed to her flippers. "I know they're

awkward, but you'll get used to them." He smiled at her. "Do you need me to help you in?"

She nodded.

"Okay." He turned and slipped over the side. She looked at the others. Everyone else was in the water already snorkeling. The bright blue water. Who knew what swam way down below them? Sweat rolled down her forehead from sitting in the sun trying to get her nerve up.

Nate swam near the Rhino Rider. His hand reached up and patted the inflatable side of the boat. "Sit here and swing your legs over the side."

She did as he instructed. The boat bobbled in the water. This wasn't so bad sitting here, but she still had to jump in.

Nate watched her. "How well do you know how to swim?"

"I was in the timid non-swimmers class every week for six months taking lessons but that feels like a long time ago. I haven't swum since and I've never been in the ocean before."

"It will come back to you."

"I'm phobic," she whispered, blinking away tears.

His hand closed over her ankle. "Kara," he commanded in a firm but gentle voice, "trust me. Give me your hand. I won't let any harm come to you."

She wanted to, she really did. Her breathing came faster, her phobia threatened to overtake her the more she sat there. Sitting on this tiny machine in the ocean was the worst place for her to have a panic attack. The edges of it raced in on her.

She wanted to snorkel with Nate. She just didn't know if she could.

"Stop thinking. Take a deep breath and take my hand."

# CHAPTER TEN

*K*ara reached her hand out. His warm hand grasped hers. He'd scuba dived all over the world. He wouldn't let anything bad happen to her. She made the leap, her gaze locked on his.

He held her in the water and didn't let her sink under.

She couldn't keep her legs still from nervousness. She licked her lips and tasted salt from the splash she made.

He still held her hand. "Try to relax. Hold still and float."

She couldn't. Her legs wouldn't stop moving. All her nervous energy drove them. Nate moved behind her, releasing her hand and slipped one arm around her waist.

She gasped. *Oh God.*

"Hold still now. Breathe." He spoke near her ear and his mouth grazed her earlobe, sending tingles down her spine. "I've got you. Relax, let yourself get used to the water."

Her legs moved with a will of their own, so he pulled her backward until she rested in his lap. Her legs finally stopped moving. If she'd thought they were close on the Rhino Rider, it was nothing compared to this. With his hard body behind her and his strong arms around her, she felt safe enough to float.

"Just float," he added in a low tone. "Relax. Breathe."

His breath in her ear sent ripples of tingles down her spine and another kind of tension began. But he held her like this was the most natural thing in the world.

"Shh, I got you, sweetheart."

They floated and she relaxed. She watched the others already snorkeling, their heads bobbing up and down in the water, having fun. Nate was so patient with her.

He gave her a slight squeeze. "Better now?"

"Yes," she breathed.

"Good." He spoke the word and she closed her eyes, the sun warming her face, soaking in the moment. If only they could stay this way.

"Ready?" He asked.

*If only he knew how ready. He could hold her like this any time.*

Kara opened her eyes. "Yes, I'm ready."

"Pull down your goggles."

She pulled them over her eyes and nose and panicked for a moment, unable to draw breath, then remembered she was supposed to breathe through her mouth.

"How's the seal?" He looked close. "Here, let me adjust those for you."

She looked through the goggles, breathing through mouth and feeling like an alien bug.

He reached around her and tightened the strap, his mouth inches from hers, and grinned. "That's better."

She smiled and blushed.

"Now the mouthpiece. Breathe through like this, not through your nose."

She put it in her mouth just as he had; his steady gaze bore into her in silent expectation.

*I don't want to let him down. I want to do this.*

It was time to put her face in the water, something she hadn't learned how to do even in the swim class. Opening her eyes under water brought on severe panic. It went better for her if she kept them closed.

As a scuba diver, Nate probably thought it no big deal and he'd think she was a big baby. She couldn't help it. She didn't know why she panicked in the water or how to make it go away.

That panic threatened to return even now.

Nate grasped her hand.

"Try it. I've got you." His fingers squeezed to reassure. "I won't let you go. Just try."

She tried not to hyperventilate, breathing slowly and deep through the mouthpiece as she put her face under.

Her heart raced as she put her face in with eyes wide open.

She forgot every worry in her mind.

A turquoise world greeted her below. Waving ocean plants and coral. A royal blue fish with a yellow stripe swam lazily by them; hundreds of tiny black fish sped beneath her flippers startling her. She popped her head out of the water and gasped.

Nate had been watching her and they removed their mouthpieces simultaneously.

"So, was it as good as I promised?"

"Better." She laughed. "I did it! Did you see them? I never dreamed it would be so wonderful."

"That's only a taste. I'll show you more if you'll let me."

She nodded, her eyes shining.

Nate held her hand, never letting go as they swam past multi-colored coral and hundreds of fish of all sizes.

Kara had never seen anything like this underwater world. The fish were so brightly colored, so unusual. Several times she tried to speak, to tell Nate something before forgetting he couldn't hear her with the mouthpiece. They pointed and communicated with their eyes. His hand never left hers. She drank in the comfort and felt safe and alive.

He motioned to her, asking her if she wanted to go down further but she shook her head no. It was one thing to float on top of the water with her head in and quite another to swim down below. What she'd accomplished probably didn't seem like much to him, but to her, it was a huge step.

When it was time to go, they swam back to the Rhino Rider. He helped remove her mask, now caught in her long hair. He pulled the golden strands loose and traced his fingertip across her lips, which tingled beneath his touch.

A wave crashed over them, surprising them both. She swallowed salt water. Choking and coughing, she reached out for him, touching his chest.

"Hey, Kara." His voice soothed as he pulled her close. "It's all right. I've got you."

She started to speak, but he kissed the top of her nose.

"It's time to go." Huskiness lingered in his tone.

If only they didn't have to.

"I know." She sighed.

*Moments of joy could bloom. But they didn't last. Any*

*more than red roses did. Then you had only the memories of what was to hold.*

"Kara." The timber of his voice called her mind back from where it hovered. "If I get out first, I can pull you out of the water. But you'll have to float for a minute by yourself."

She nodded, and he let go. As soon as he did, she began kicking. Without him to hold onto, she couldn't hold her legs still.

He pulled himself out and removed his gear quickly. "See if you can take off your flippers first."

She struggled with her flippers in the water while the others climbed out of the sea, but she got them off. He took them, stuck them in the side of the Rhino Rider, and then held his hands out to her. "Grab hold."

She reached up.

He grasped her hands, lifted her out, and plopped her on the side of the boat.

She had no idea he was so strong.

He smoothed wet strands of hair off her forehead with a gentle hand. "Are you ready to head back?"

"As ready as I'll ever be. I wish we could stay."

"Me too." He smiled. "But I'm looking forward to taking you dancing tonight."

"I wouldn't want to be anywhere else."

*Than in your arms.*

She didn't finish the statement out loud but the wish went up.

"I'm glad, Kara. You're very special to me." His finger stroked under her chin and he bent to kiss her, his lips brushing hers slowly and tenderly.

When he pulled away, giving her a deep smile, she realized what a gift he'd given her today. More than just teaching her to snorkel, he reminded her what it was to be alive. Alive under this blue Caribbean sky, the aqua water below them full of life.

She looked around, soaking everything in. Her job at the bank seemed far away and lifeless. A dead end. She'd been at that dead calm ever since Neil died, when nothing had moved forward again.

Until Nate.

The drivers started the engines. Kara slipped her hands around Nate's waist again, and they sped toward the pier. Her hair flew in the wind, and this time she chanced fully facing the sights they passed. It made her laugh. She'd missed so much hiding away behind him on the way there.

They reached the pier too soon and turned in the machines and gear. A photographer stood by the entrance to the Rhino Rider hut selling photos of all the couples on the boats. He had taken pictures before they raced away, but she'd been preoccupied.

"Do you want one?" Nate lifted theirs to look at it.

"No, that's okay." She didn't want to seem sappy. The photo showed her head burrowing against his back, as she pressed close against him. He wore a big grin.

"I'll take it," He told the photographer. He turned to Kara. "I'd like one and they come in pairs. Here." He handed her one of the photos. "Something to remember the day."

"Thank you."

*What a nice gift. He looked strong and sexy in that photo. I'll always treasure this photo and the memory of today.*

She wondered if she'd spend hours looking at the photo and missing him when she was home again.

Nate paid the man for the photo then they boarded the van.

Kara stretched her towel across the seat. Salty seawater and sticky suntan lotion covered her. Everyone wore swimsuits back, trying to dry off.

Nate stretched his arm across the back of her seat. She studied his profile as he chatted with the others about the black coral reef none of them would have seen had he not taken the initiative. Confidence rolled off of him with everything he did. His black hair looked silky and gleamed from the seawater. She longed to touch it.

They rode back to the ship and the van stopped to let them off. Daryl approached, tossing the newspaper he'd either been reading or hiding behind into the trash, and Kara quickly rewrapped her towel around her waist as he drew near.

Nate placed his hand on the small of Kara's back and they moved forward together.

Daryl stopped in front of her, his feet spread in a strong stance, "Kara, I want a word with you." The straw hat he now wore partially hid his expression, making her nervous as to what he wanted and what his mood was.

"If you want me to get rid of him for you just say the word," Nate said under his breath.

"No," she whispered, "He's my boss."

Nate didn't say another word, but she sensed tension coiled within his body.

"Daryl, I have to get ready for dinner."

"I've been here waiting for you for some time. You can give me ten minutes." His gaze dropped to her red bikini top then up to her face again.

Kara frowned in confusion as they moved toward the ship and he continued to walk on the other side of her from Nate. "But I told you I didn't know when we'd be back."

Daryl acted like she had done something wrong, but she hadn't agreed to meet him again. It wasn't her fault he'd waited. Why was he acting like she was to blame?

Kara didn't like the way his eyes had lit as he looked at her breasts in the brief moment before the shadow of the hat hid his eyes again or the fact he'd seen her in a bikini top.

It gave her a squirmish feeling, even with Nate right beside her.

"We have things to discuss. You can spare me ten minutes before you go."

As Nate guided her toward the ship, forcing Daryl to walk alongside, Nate's words to her during snorkeling came back to her, *I've got you.*

"Daryl, I have to go. I'll see you at work when I get home. Enjoy your visit to the island."

They reached the gangplank.

Daryl stepped forward and Kara froze.

"I can't believe you're being so cold. And rude."

Pressure from Nate's hand and his presence next to her made her feel bold. She wasn't going to stay here and talk to him. This was her vacation and he did not belong in it.

"I'm not the one being rude. I didn't show up unannounced on someone else's vacation and expect them to drop everything for me."

She hurried up the gangplank with Nate right beside her and she didn't look back.

"I wish you had let me take care of him for you." Nate's voice was quiet and calm but there lay anger beneath it. "I'd make sure he never bothered you again."

Kara's hands shook as she placed her beach bag on the conveyer for the security guards to scan before they entered the ship again. "The problem is I have to work with him."

"Sweetheart, are you all right?"

She walked through the metal detector, turning to wait for him to walk through and join her. "Yes, Nate. But I'm a little worried about my job. This whole day has been so..."

He pulled her close, listening and watching the conflicting expressions cross her face.

"It's been one of the best days and also one of the worst days of my life. I wish we could have stayed out there in the water and never came back. I'm dreading going home now."

"I can understand that."

They stepped into the elevator. The press of people pushed them back into the corner.

"I don't want him ruining my cruise."

He slid his arm around her waist pulling her close and kissed her temple. "Forget about him. Tonight is the Captain's dinner."

"Yes." She smiled.

"There's my happy woman." He smiled back at her.

"Are you wearing a tux tonight?"

"Of course, sweetheart."

Oh, she could imagine him in a tux, dark hair and tanned, those deep brown eyes and that wonderful smile. *He would be so handsome.*

All thoughts of Daryl fled as her mind filled with

images. Thanks to Viv, some of those images were of him taking that tux off while she watched.

Once out of the elevator, he walked her to her cabin and kissed her softly on the lips.

Nate raised his head and looked down at her. "Call my room when you're ready and I'll escort you to dinner."

She smiled. "All right."

He winked as she opened her door and he took off down the hall.

Viv was in the shower already, but she had pulled clothes and jewelry out and strewn them all over the bed and dresser. It was as if she didn't have to share the room. She'd taken over all available spaces except Kara's bed.

*How terribly selfish.*

Viv stepped out of the bathroom. "Nate has got a bonnie bum, that he does."

*What is it with her and my boyfriend? Doesn't she have enough boyfriends of her own? Including that nice British man who taught her all those expressions.*

"Will you stop with the British expressions? You're driving me mad."

"That's a British expression, driving me mad, and I like them. I wouldn't say them if I didn't like them."

Kara rolled her eyes in exasperation. *At least Viv was in a better mood now. It would be nice if she would keep it till the end of the cruise.*

She noticed a red box with a gold bow out of the

corner of her eye that had been placed on her bed. "Where did that come from?"

"Where do you think?" Viv laughed. "Good show, Nate."

Kara sat on the bed to open the box, which was addressed to her. She pulled off the gold ribbon and lifted the lid. Peeling back red tissue paper, she gasped.

Viv laughed as she looked over Kara's shoulder. "Girl, you're gonna love those."

Kara's jaw dropped and her eyes widened. She reached into the box and lifted out a pair of red, strawberry flavored, edible panties. "Oh wow."

She sat on the bed, stunned.

"Don't get yourself in a muddle. Look, there's a card."

Kara opened it and read "Nothing could be sweeter than sharing the evening with you."

"Go Nate." Viv smirked.

"I wonder why he didn't sign it?"

"Who cares? Tell him to eat through the middle first."

Kara turned beat red but didn't laugh. "Nate doesn't strike me as the type of guy to leave his name off a card." She frowned.

"Yeah, he's more a name it and claim it kind a guy."

Kara sat holding them, intrigued. She'd heard of

edible panties but never held a pair. "I wonder if they taste good?"

"Take a nibble."

They both laughed and Kara relaxed. "No, I don't think so."

"Well, you're not the one who'll be eating them." Viv laughed again.

*Edible panties. Did he get them on the island? The stores on the ship didn't sell things like that. Did they?*

Did he want her to wear them tonight? She wasn't ready. *This was moving too fast.* She needed to talk to him. And this was the Captain's Dinner, a formal evening. She'd wear silk stockings, not edible underwear.

*Goodness, what could he be thinking? Surely he doesn't expect me to wear them to dinner tonight? This is total surprise. We need to talk about this.*

She pulled on lace panties and then silk stockings. After stepping into a black satin evening dress, she stood in front of the mirror. The dress fit close and the open back dipped all the way down to her lower back. She'd never worn anything so revealing and tonight she felt like the most desirable woman in the world. In fact she felt delicious. All the talk and teasing he'd been doing about food and eating had sent her thoughts in this direction. Even more so since receiving the gift. He'd made it clear there was at least one thing he'd like to do with her. She felt delicious and naughty.

Viv dressed in a purple sequined gown. She turned to look at Kara. "Girl, I can't believe you're wearing that. So daring and sexy."

Kara glanced into the mirror. She paused and wished for the first time in her life that someone could paint her. Just like this.

She'd never really seen herself before. Vital. Alive. Beautiful.

Viv sniffed. "If that's new perfume, I don't care for it."

"It's not new. Neil's mother gave it to me."

"The woman hates you."

"Yes, well, she doesn't hate me, but she didn't like me much before and now she blames me for his death."

"I wouldn't wear that if I were you."

*Maybe she needed to cleanse her life of some remnants Neil left behind. Including gifts from his mother.*

This wasn't her old life now. She could choose a new perfume to celebrate her new life.

Kara washed her hands and wrists in the sink. She hadn't yet sprayed it behind her ears where she couldn't wash it off. She lifted the perfume bottle and dropped it in the trash.

"I called the guys and said we'd meet them at the cocktail party."

"But Nate was going to meet me here." Disappointment filled her. "He was going to escort me."

"Plans changed."

Viv had made plans without consulting her. Kara frowned, wondering what had been said to pull that off. "Let's go then."

They headed to the Captain's Cocktail Party in the theater.

Her earrings swung whenever Kara turned her head. They almost touched her shoulders, and she'd left her hair down. She felt like a fashion model on parade as men watched her move.

Nate let out a long, low, approving whistle as she approached. Nate in a black tux made her weak in the knees. The way he filled out the tux with his broad shoulders and the shine in his dark hair and dark eyes. His gaze held her still. A slow grin began in the corner of his mouth and spread across his face, his white smile even brighter contrasted by his tan and the black tux.

Warmth flooded through her. She needed a chair. Or a fan. She resisted the urge to fan herself with her hand. "You look marvelous this evening, sweetheart," Nate said, moving toward her to take her hands in his. "I admit the extra time to get ready seemed unnecessary because you're beautiful without makeup. But looking at you now..." He held her away from him, their hands touching and his gaze swept her again from head to toe. "You look good enough to eat."

His deep voice sent a ripple of awareness

through her body and she thought about the strawberry panties.

"Thank you." Flustered and suddenly shy, she didn't know what else to say.

*Good enough to eat. Oh my.* Her face turned what she knew must be a bright shade of red. *Could he think I'm wearing the strawberry panties now?*

With great effort, she turned her gaze away from him to scan the room. A champagne fountain stood in the middle of the room. Waiters walked about with trays of champagne. She accepted a glass from a passing waiter and turned back to Nate.

His deep brown eyes watched her and his expression told her he found her beautiful, as much as his words had done. Women dressed in sequins and beads, diamonds and elegant gowns filled the room, yet he paid them little attention.

His hand slipped behind her back. She breathed in as his fingers touched the small of her back.

"Chilled?"

She was, but the heat from his fingers warmed her. "Only a little."

He leaned close and whispered in her ear. "I'm glad it's just the two of us tonight. This is going to be a magical evening, Kara. I'm glad we'll be bringing in the New Year together."

His breath tickled her ear sending tingles down her spine as she thought of the edible panties again.

*Yes, it was.* She would give herself up to his kisses, his touch and let this night be an evening to remember.

# CHAPTER ELEVEN

*hampagne before dinner on an empty stomach can go to your head quick,* Kara noted.

She'd passed up *hors d'oeuvres*, afraid to ruin her appetite before dinner, and now her stomach butterflies filled her stomach. She couldn't keep the smile off of her face. The smile was as much from the idea of the edible panties waiting in her room as the champagne.

*Oh, these long menus.*

The menus were doing her in. Or was it Nate's knee touching hers under the table?

*There are all these fancy dishes tonight. How can any woman focus while thoughts of strawberry panties for desert run through her head?*

*For the Captain's Gala Dinner,* the menu read, *Caspian Seuruga Malossol Caviar on ice throne with American Dressing, Liver Pate Strasbourg, Petite*

Marmite Henry IV, Eleonora Salad with Balsamic Dressing, Tournedos of Beef Tenderloin Montmorency--

She stopped. Just reading a partial list made her dizzy.

*Why does every dish have to have a fancy name?*

She reached for a roll and leaned toward Nate.

"Pass the butter please."

"Here you are, sweetheart." His intense but tender gaze melted her like butter.

Nate's knee brushed hers then lingered as he leaned down to the floor.

*What's he doing? Oh, he dropped his napkin.*

His gaze moved up her body past her breasts as he sat up with the napkin. His eyes sparkled with mischief. "Chilly, sweetheart?"

"No. I'm warm."

*It's so warm in here. Warm enough to dump a pitcher of water over my overheated body.* She fanned herself with the menu.

*Oh, dear. Too much champagne and no food.*

The waiter approached again, wanting her order. She, as usual, wasn't ready.

*Why does this happen every time I have dinner with him?*

"Uh, soup." *No, too hot for soup.* "No. Scratch that. Fruit cup instead."

"And for the main course?"

Her mind went blank, and she had to look at the

menu again. "Lobster or Salmon sound good. Which is better?"

"You could always order both," Nate said.

"Yes, both. Why not?"

*That made things easier.*

She laid down the menu.

"And for a side dish?"

"Potatoes." *Whatever kind they have tonight.*

The waiter read back her selections and she nodded, glad to be done. She watched the slow way Nate spread butter over his roll. The thought of his long fingers on her skin started the butterflies inside flitting again.

Her stomach growled, and he glanced up and offered her his roll.

"Thank you."

"You're welcome."

She nibbled on the roll as she watched him butter another roll and willed the butterflies to stop.

As the courses were served, her mouth watered and she focused on them. She couldn't believe how hungry she was. Everything looked and tasted so good.

"It's good to see you enjoying your food," Nate said. "Fresh air and exercise build up quite an appetite." He winked.

Kara froze with her fork halfway to her mouth. Butter dripped off the lobster portion impaled there. *Appetite. Was he referring to the panties?* "Oh, yes," Kara said, turning beet red. She finished taking the bite and watched Nate eat. Every bite he took made her think of his mouth on her panties. Nate's gaze traveled across her face, neck and shoulders, which felt warmer as the evening went on.

"You got a lot of sun today."

"Yes. Maybe too much."

"You'll need a stronger sun block or to apply more often when we're out on or in the water. The sun here is stronger than you may realize and the ocean wears the sun block away."

"Thank you. I'll pick a stronger bottle."

The waiter approached. "Are you ready to order desert?"

Her gaze flew to Nate as she answered. "I'll pass on dessert for now. I'm not ready for that right now."

*They needed to talk.* Would he understand her meaning? That she was referring to the edible underpants waiting in her room?

Nate's warm hand closed over hers, sending a tingle up her arm. Her heart raced and the room grew even warmer.

"That was a filling meal. I believe I'll pass on desert too." He gave her a smile and she relaxed.

"Would you care to go for a walk around the deck?" Nate's fingertips did a slow trace across her hand.

"Yes. I'd like that. I'm too full to do much else."

"We have all evening." He winked.

She blushed and grew warmer yet.

"We won't stay out long but the fresh air will be good."

"Yes, I, I could use some fresh air. It's so warm in here."

"Then shall we?" He stood and pulled out her chair, and they said good night to Viv and Adam, who stayed for desert.

Outside the cool wind blew. Her backless dress wasn't warm enough, despite her sun kissed skin that was turning warmer and redder as the evening went on.

Nate pulled her close. Kara slid her arms around his waist. She snuggled in closer, her breasts against his warm body.

He bent and kissed her ear. "Better now, sweetheart?" His warm breath against her skin spread tingles down her back.

"Yes," she nodded. "I was feeling overly warm inside. But the wind is cool."

"You feel good, sweetheart. All soft and warm." He kissed her neck. "And you taste delicious."

Her body threatened to turn into a pool of molten lava at any moment.

*Delicious. Oh, yes. I am.*

She gave a low sexy laugh. One she didn't know she had.

His tongue on her ear caused her to think of other places his tongue could go. Places much lower.

He kissed her earlobe, behind her ear, her neck, and a bit lower down as if he followed the direction of her thoughts.

She breathed in each time he placed another kiss on her heated skin. A gust of wind came and goose bumps pebbled across her skin. He stopped kissing her even as her body said *no, don't stop.*

"Let's get out of this wind," he said.

"All right," she said. Though she really wanted the kissing to continue.

They went back in, holding hands and strolling slowly.

Every bar on the ship blared one form of music or another, and even the old folks were dressed for partying to bring in the New Year. Kara and Nate passed a bar where a man crooned an old Dean Martin song at the piano bar.

"Let's go in here till it's time for the midnight buffet," Nate said.

"Oh, yes. I love the piano and he's playing so well."

They listened to a few numbers, but soon it was time to head to the gala midnight buffet. In the grand dining room the maître d' sprayed a mountain of wineglasses down with a light spray of champagne while standing on a tall stool. He poured from the first bottle into the upper most glass. Soon champagne flowed down the tower.

When the fountain was ready and the musicians had taken their places, the captain welcomed them all to the midnight buffet. Musicians began to play.

The countdown to the New Year began.

Kara's heart pounded as she looked up at Nate, watching his lips as he whispered the countdown.

*Ten.* Her mouth felt dry and she moistened her lips.

*Nine.* He smiled and she returned his smile.

*Eight.* She felt giddy.

*Seven.* She counted with him.

*Six.* He watched her lips and his eyes lit.

*Five.* Almost there.

*Four.* Remember this kiss.

*Three.* He drew closer.

*Two.* Her lips parted.

*One.*

People cheered the New Year all around them, glasses tinkling in toasts.

He pressed his lips to hers, caressing, softly teasing with his tongue as her lips parted wider, giving herself over to the passion of the moment. She wanted more, wanted to give him more, wanted this to be a kiss to remember. Her hands threaded through his hair at the back of his neck, pulling him closer. He deepened the kiss. His hands pressed against the small of her back, bringing her hips next to him. She wanted him close, wanted all of him. Her breathing grew ragged as her whole body responded. The kiss was urgent, hungry, and passionate.

He broke the kiss, and they came up for air. Raising his mouth from hers, he gazed into her eyes. Still he held her close, smiling. "You're so beautiful."

Nate touched her as if she were a treasure, with tenderness in his gaze.

"I feel beautiful tonight."

"As you should, always."

He bent and kissed her again, this time a light, teasing kiss. His mood seemed light. His tongue tickled her lips and her tongue, making her smile.

He pulled back again. "Much as I'd enjoy kissing you all night, you wanted to take pictures of the food displays."

"Yes," she smiled. "I did. And we haven't had desert yet."

Camera flashes went off all over the room as people took photos.

Kara had never seen anything like it. There were carved ice swans and an eagle with wings spread. A swordfish out of ice. Then there were the chocolate sculptures. A ship with sails, a bear, a cowboy riding a bucking horse. The culinary artists carved fruits and vegetables into other arrangements, and desert after desert for passengers to enjoy surrounded the arrangements.

Nate slid his arm around her waist. "Glad you waited?"

"Oh, yes," she breathed. "Good things are always worth waiting for."

"Yes, they are." He smiled.

Anticipation along with the sound of his voice had her all a tingle. She loved the way he teased her without ever hinting at his gift.

They got in line and moved down each row. She put key lime pie on her plate and chocolate covered strawberries. He went for the cheesecake and a slice of rich chocolate cake.

"That looks good," she said, "But I could never eat a whole slice. It's too rich."

"I'll share with you, sweetheart."

The thought of what they would share later on made her blush.

"You're so pretty when you blush"

Of course this made her blush even more. "It's my pale coloring."

"Well, I like it."

She laughed that low sexy laugh again, thinking of how much she'd blush when he saw her in those panties.

They found a table in a quiet corner by themselves and a waiter came by with more champagne. They turned it down and asked for coffee instead.

She took a bite of the pie and closed her eyes.

"I love a woman who enjoys her food."

She opened her eyes and smiled at him. "Key lime pie is my favorite."

"I'll remember that."

He offered her a piece of chocolate cake. "Bite?"

"Yes." She opened her mouth and he slid it in. "Mmm."

He watched with a smile. "I enjoy feeding you, sweetheart."

She laughed, feeling bolder and quite naughty. "I hope you'll let me return the favor."

"Of course."

She picked up one of the strawberries and held it out, imagining his mouth closing over her fingers.

"Sorry sweetheart, no strawberries for me." He shook his head. "I'm allergic."

"What?" She frowned. "Allergic?"

"Yes."

*Oh my God. He didn't send them.*

Her stomach flipped.

"Kara? Sweetheart, what's wrong?"

"You didn't send them," she whispered, as the hand holding the strawberry dropped it, sinking to the table, the berry rolling off and onto the floor.

## CHAPTER TWELVE

$\mathcal{N}$ ate grasped both Kara's cool, limp hands as she stared at him in horror, the chill coming up over her sun kissed back.

*If he didn't send them, then who?*

The shock hit her hard.

*Daryl.*

"Kara?"

His warm hands rubbed hers. "Sweetheart, talk to me. I didn't send what?"

She forced the words out in a low whisper. "Edible panties."

"What?" He frowned.

She whispered again. "Someone sent me edible panties, but the card wasn't signed."

"And you thought I sent them."

"Yes. But they're strawberry, so you didn't..." Her voice trailed off as she closed her eyes before opening them again to look at him. "You didn't send them."

Nick's face turned from concern to an angry frown. Anger radiated off of him.

"No, I didn't send them but I'd sure as hell like to know who did."

He let loose of her hands and clenched his own as he dropped them out of sight below the table. "It had to be your boss."

She wanted it to be Nate and hadn't entertained the thought it could be anyone else. "I haven't been on a date since Neil died. Until I met you." She pursed her lips, thinking.

"It was Daryl," Nate's tone left no doubt.

*It had to be Daryl. Who else? But ... he wouldn't do something so inappropriate. Would he?* She hesitated. "No, he wouldn't do something like this."

Nate's hands clenched. "Don't be so sure."

"Well, I don't have any proof it was him."

She couldn't believe Daryl would step over the line like this. He *had* flown to a Caribbean island and interrupted her cruise. That fact was still hard to take in.

She frowned.

Nate stood, the force of the move pushing his chair back. "Let's find your room steward. Whoever sent it, he delivered it. Don't worry sweetheart. I'll get to the bottom of this."

They left their deserts and tracked down the

room steward, who had just come out of another stateroom. He said he'd make inquiries and let them know. Any package could be delivered once it was scanned and cleared through security, but the ship didn't sell edible panties. He seemed offended at the question.

After the room steward left to check, Kara let Nate into her room and handed him the box. He read the card, frowned, and turned it over, but the other side was blank.

"He planned ahead. He purchased it off the ship, had it wrapped and delivered. This wasn't spontaneous. This was planned."

Kara frowned. "This is crazy."

"Yes, it is."

*Oh my God. Crazy out of control things happened all the time when you least expect them. Neil's death is proof of that. The trick is to always be prepared so they won't jump out at you. But how can you prepare for this?*

She hadn't been prepared. No, she'd ventured out of her comfort zone to go on this cruise and now look what had happened.

"Kara?" Nate placed his arm around her shoulder and rubbed it, warming her. "Sweetheart, you're a million miles away. What are you thinking about?"

"I don't like this." She looked up into his eyes. "I'm really uncomfortable with the way Daryl has been behaving. But I have no proof he sent these and he'll just deny it."

"We're going to get to the bottom of this, sweetheart. Don't worry. I'll see to it." He opened his arms and she moved into them. His arms closed around her. "I've got you. It's going to be all right."

He rubbed her back, sending the chills away, warming her. The anticipation, which had built up all evening, fled with the discovery he hadn't sent the gift. Now she only wanted him to hold her, safe and warm within his arms. The chemistry between them that sizzled held a back seat to the comfort he offered her now, the comfort she needed.

She inhaled his scent and listened to his calm voice. There was just something about him that kept her fears at bay when he was near.

"Do you still want to go dancing?"

"Not yet."

She wanted to stay here in his arms. She wanted that safe, warm feeling she felt inside his arms. She dared not think the word forever.

"I could hold you all night, sweetheart."

NATE HADN'T INTENDED on falling so hard for Kara. He hadn't intended on getting this attached to any woman. But Kara kept drawing him in and the more he knew her, the more he wanted to know her in every way.

When he held her in his arms, happiness spread

through him in a way he couldn't have explained to anyone. It was foolish to feel this way. A shipboard romance could turn out like all his other relationships. Every woman he'd fallen in love with had turned out to be the wrong one, either cheating on him or leaving him when he needed her. Then he'd move on, never willing to settle for less than true love.

This beautiful, fearful woman in his arms needed his protection. The sense that she belonged in his arms, like a puzzle piece that fit, came over him every time he held her. She needed him, though she didn't ask for help. Unlike some women's needy manipulative games, this was a real need and yet she never once used it to manipulate. She was guileless and truthful. Innocent in ways few women her age were.

He'd find whoever sent those damn panties. *Everything pointed to Daryl, whether she could see that or not.* There was no one else it could be since she hadn't been dating anyone.

Nate inhaled her scent, enjoying every minute of holding her so near, but hating that fear made her reach for him. He didn't want her to be afraid, ever.

She wasn't the only one frightened by the chain of events. He'd never fallen so fast, hard and deep for a woman. And that made him nervous as hell.

She'd quieted. He pulled her down to sit on the

bed with him and cupped the side of her face. "Better?"

She nodded and he saw the exhaustion in her face. "Yes."

"You're tired. I'll go so you can sleep."

She only nodded again but didn't speak.

He gave her a soft kiss and stood. "We both need sleep. Would you like to look around St. Thomas later?"

"Yes, I'd like that."

"Good. Sweet dreams, sweetheart. Nothing but sweet dreams for you. Call me when you wake up."

"Okay, I will."

He let himself out.

AFTER THEY SLEPT, which wasn't nearly enough sleep for either of them after bringing in the New Year, Kara met Nate for a late lunch, where she nibbled at her food and pushed it around on her plate. The misunderstanding the night before had stolen her appetite. The dining room sun glinted through the windows, making her squint.

Everything seemed so bright after the late night bringing in the New Year. Through large windows on one side she saw the island of St. Thomas.

"Hung over?" Nate asked.

"No." She paused. "Well, maybe a little."

"If you're not feeling up to exploring the island, we can skip it."

"No. I want to go look through the shops."

*I'll buy something cheerful for myself. Maybe something yellow.* She loved yellow. It was so cheerful.

The ships photographer snapped their picture at the end of the gangplank, as they seemed to do every time passengers disembarked onto a port of call. Later they'd try to sell them the photos in the photo galleries before dinner, but Kara had yet to go look at any of those pictures.

St. Thomas bustled with shoppers from four cruise ships docked in the harbor. Old warehouses once used by pirates to store their goods made a picturesque setting and the people wore colorful clothing as they bustled about.

"Here comes the donkey mon," called a young boy.

A man wearing dreadlocks and multicolored clothes led a donkey down the middle of the street. Kara laughed. The donkey wore large pink plastic sunglasses and a Santa hat.

The man stopped. "Pretty lady. You want de picture taken wit dees donkey mon? Five dolla."

"Yes." She nodded.

*How silly. How fun.*

She stood by the donkey "mon" and his donkey and motioned for Nate to join her.

"Okay." He laughed.

They smiled for the photo his young helper snapped with a Polaroid camera, then the man printed it out and she gave him five dollars, shaking her head at Nate when he tried to pay.

The rest of the afternoon they wandered through the shops. She bought a yellow sundress along with a black and yellow striped silk scarf and small dangling banana earrings. Nate bought a book on nautical adventures in the historical section of the bookstore, and Kara picked up a romance set in Scotland. Satisfied with their shopping, they headed back to the ship.

In her stateroom Kara emptied her bags onto the bed while Viv flipped through a magazine she'd picked up.

"Are you on a yellow kick or something? That scarf doesn't go with that sundress," Viv said.

"The scarf is for when I wear black to work."

"Yeah, you have all those boring bank clothes."

"Well, you don't have to worry about my boring clothes. I've decided yellow will be my signature color."

Viv rolled her eyes. "Okay, whatever. Hey, Adam bought tickets for the Kon Tiki Party Boat. It's a glass bottom boat, nothing but relaxation and rum punch. I told Adam I need rest after we had it away last night."

"Had it away?"

Viv wiggled her eyebrows. "You know."

*Uh. She's at it again with the British expressions. Maybe if Viv spends more time with Adam she'll stop all that. It just sounds silly in someone who's not British.*

Kara reached into her bag. "Wait till you see the photo I had taken with the 'donkey mon.'" She rummaged and pulled it out. "Look."

Viv took one look and burst out laughing. "You had your picture taken with an ass."

Kara looked at the photo. She and Nate stood beside the donkey smiling with joy and the Rasta man, smiling, his teeth white against his dark as night skin.

"Way to go, Kara," Viv handed the photo back. "You can tell people you sailed to the Caribbean and met an ass."

*I didn't have to sail to an island to meet one. I'm sharing a room with one now. What is wrong with her? Why can't she be happy I'm happy?*

Kara put the photo away. "I'm going out. See you later."

"Later."

She was tired of Viv and needed to get out of their tiny cabin before she blew up.

The stateroom phone rang and Viv answered. "Hello, Adam? Oh. Yes, she's here." She handed the phone to Kara. "Nate."

162

"Thank you." Kara took the phone. "Hello."

"Hello, sweetheart. Want to go on the Kon Tiki party boat? They've got two tickets left but I have to buy them now. The boat leaves in forty five minutes."

"Yes, I'd like that."

"You'll need to wear a swimsuit. The boat stops in a cove for swimming and volleyball. And bring a towel."

"Okay. Where do you want to meet?"

Viv went out the door without so much as a wave.

"The ticket office?"

"See you there."

Kara hung up the phone, changed, and hurried to meet him.

"Hello, sweetheart." He reached for her and wrapped his arms around her.

"Hello," she said.

He bent to give her a quick kiss, and then he pulled away and took her hand. "You ready?"

"Yes."

He squeezed her hand and they walked off the ship and down to where the tour met. Even boarding the large Kon Tiki party boat, he didn't let go of her hand for a minute.

Kara sat on the bench that ran along the side of the boat and Nate sat down beside her. Captain Muldoon welcomed everyone on board and introduced the steel band. The band played calypso music as the ship slowly sailed away from the pier and passengers lined up at the bar for drinks.

A soft breeze blew. Kara watched out of the corner of her eye how Nate's dark hair ruffled in the breeze, and he watched her with a smile.

"Hey, Kara. I missed you." His warm smile could melt an iceberg.

She smiled back at him. "I missed you too."

He stretched his arm across the back of her bench, and she caught the scent of aftershave mingled with suntan lotion.

They passed a large inflated Santa on one of the docks.

"Caribbean Santa wears sunglasses and a grass skirt," Kara said.

Nate laughed. "There were enough of those Caribbean Santas in the shops."

"Yes, there were." Almost every shop had at least one Caribbean Santa ornament. "Must be where Santa goes on vacation once Christmas is over."

As they sailed along, a crewman removed a wooden platform in the middle of the boat so passengers could see through the glass bottom. But the fish were fewer and less colorful than the ones Kara saw while snorkeling with Nate. A week ago she'd have found this excursion exciting. Now it seemed quiet and uneventful. Though after the events of yesterday that was a good thing.

"Mmm. You smell so good," Nate whispered low in her ear, sending that hum through her body again, his voice and words pouring over her, sinking in like the warm sunshine.

She closed her eyes, basking in it. "Thank you," she murmured.

The hum that started in anytime he came near or even said hello hummed inside her body. As his fingers rubbed her bare arm up and down the hum increased.

*If only we could be alone on this boat or on the island. I wish he would make love to me soon, before this cruise is over and I have to go back to Ohio.*

She sent the wish up and then opened her eyes again meeting his gaze.

"Hello again, day dreamer." He smiled.

"Hello again."

The boat drew up to the beach at Honeymoon Cove, and everyone stepped out onto the sand. Kara turned, taking in the scene around her. On the beach beyond the volleyball net stood a grove of trees to lounge under. Sailboats bobbed a short distance away in the beautiful, blue-green water as birds sang in the trees.

"It's like paradise," she said.

Kara spread her towel under a tree and lay down.

"Yes, it is." Nate dropped his things next to hers. "Want to join in the volleyball game?"

"No, thank you. I just want to relax." She wasn't as

athletic as Viv, who'd already joined the game with Adam.

"Okay, well, I'll be over there."

She nodded closed her eyes in the warm sun. The ocean breeze blew across her body.

*This is perfect. So restful.*

Volleyball players shouted and Nate's voice stood out. She listened for a moment then stopped thinking as sound receded into the background until she drifted off to sleep.

Even before he said a word, Kara knew Nate stood next to her. He radiated vitality that drew her like a magnet. When she opened her eyes and glanced up, her breath caught.

From this angle he was magnificent. His stance emphasized the muscular force of his thighs and the slimness of his hips. But that was nothing compared to his powerful chest and shoulders.

He dropped down beside her. The warmth of his smile echoed in his voice. "Sure you don't want to play volleyball? They're starting another game."

She found it impossible not to return his disarming smile. "I'm sure."

His gaze roved and lazily appraised her. "Okay, but if you're going to lay out, how about if I put suntan lotion on your back. You don't wanna get too much sun."

His nearness made her senses spin. Just what she needed, his hands rubbing lotion over her body, sending her into overload right here on the beach. She nodded and rolled over.

He reached for the tube and soon his warm hands glided up from the small of her back to the tops of her shoulders and down the back of her arms. He found a knot in the muscle of her shoulder blade and rubbed it out. She'd been tenser than she realized.

She exhaled into the towel as her tension eased. He turned her head to one side and then the other as he massaged her neck. His strong hands felt so good. She dug her toes down into the warm sand. Her body grew heavier and warmer. If only he'd keep rubbing. She could've gone to sleep if not for her that hum inside her crying out for more, more, more.

He stopped and she opened one eye to see him as he sat back on his heels. "That's it unless you have somewhere else you'd like me to rub."

*Oh, boy. Do I ever.* Her body ached for him to touch her again. Everywhere.

He waited and she had to find the words. Luxuriating in that warm, relaxed feeling he'd left her with, she rolled over.

"Mmm, that felt great. Thank you."

"I'm glad you enjoyed it."

"I wouldn't mind you doing that again later."

"Any time sweetheart. It would be my pleasure."

The flame smoldering in his eyes told her he

knew she wasn't just talking about putting lotion on. Again she wished they were alone.

His smile sent tingles all the way down to her sand sprinkled toes. "Want to go for a swim?"

She glanced toward the sparkling water. It looked refreshing, and she was overheated but she couldn't. "No, I don't have a life jacket."

"You don't need one. Even if you can't swim, the salt water will hold you up."

She looked at the water doubtfully, yet felt foolish for acting like such a baby.

"Trust me, Kara. You'll be fine. I wouldn't take you anywhere that wasn't safe." He held out his hand. "Come on. Aren't you getting hot? I am."

She took his hand, and he pulled her to her feet. They walked to the water's edge holding hands. He gave her a quick squeeze for reassurance before they went into the water.

Waves rolled in so gently the water barely moved, and she felt no tow at her feet. They waded in to her waist.

"Tell me when you think you've gone far enough, and I'll stop," Nate said with a low rasp in his voice.

Kara sensed he was talking about more than the water. He was a gentleman. He respected her. This made her want him even more. She wanted more than just this cruise together.

*Try not to think of that. Of how soon he'll be gone.*

He pulled her farther out until the water rose

almost to her shoulders. She halted. "Wait. Far enough."

"Try to float," he said, holding her hand. "I've got you."

Floating had been the hardest thing in her swim class, and she still couldn't do it in the deep end where she couldn't put her feet back down. Panic tried to take over, but it subsided when he squeezed her hand again.

"There's nothing to be afraid of sweetheart. Try leaning back. I've got you."

Kara drew in a deep breath and leaned back into the water. Her feet lifted, and she floated on the surface.

"There you go. Not so bad, is it?" His voice near her ear comforted her.

"It is easier to float here in this cove."

"That's because it's so salty. I'm going to let go of your hand now, but I'm right here, sweetheart."

He let go. He floated on his back beside her, looking up at the sky. "This is the best way to see clouds."

"Yes, it's beautiful." Clouds floated like cotton candy in the blue sky. "I wish I could live near a beach."

"What's stopping you?"

"I've always lived in Ohio. My house is there."

"You can find a job and a house anywhere if you

really want to," he stated as if the answer were obvious.

"I suppose."

"Some houses are nicer than others, and some jobs are better than others, but if you really want to live near a beach, you could make it happen."

He echoed her secret longings. *How did he know?*

"I suppose. But I wouldn't know anyone, and I'd have to start new with every aspect of my life."

"It's not as hard as you might think."

"For you, maybe."

*He probably picks up and moves whenever he wants. He must have women all over the world.*

He watched her measuring something. "Do you like your job?"

"It pays the bills."

"Sweetheart, there's more to life than paying the bills," he said with quiet emphasis. "There is following your passion. Doing what you love."

"I think that only happens in movies. I don't know anyone doing that. Did you like your job in the military?"

"I thrived on the rush of it for years. Until I got out and went into the scuba diving business. So yes, I guess I would say yes. And I'm happy scuba diving and being out on the water. I'm in my element in the water."

Listening to him she realized how comfortable

she'd become with him in such a short period of time.

He didn't feel like someone she'd just met, but like someone she'd known and somehow forgotten. As if he'd been waiting for her to find him or for him to find her. As if she could tell him absolutely anything and he would not only listen, he would hear her fully. The things said and the things unsaid.

*Meeting him and talking to him feel like coming home. And this was very real. No fairy tale wishful thinking.*

*Viv was wrong about men. Wrong about a lot of things.* The time for listening to Viv's council had passed. Even if it had happened fast, this was more than just a shipboard fling. But as wonderful as things were with Nate; the cruise would end very soon and if she never saw him again...

The thought made her heart hurt.

"What's worrying you, sweetheart?"

Over at the Kon Tiki the captain called everyone to board before she could think of an answer.

"I'll collect your stuff. Go on and swim over to the boat," he said as if it was the most normal thing in the world for her to do.

*Swim by myself and no flotation?*

He gave her a look that said she could do it, and winked before turning toward the beach and heading for her towel and beach bag.

The panic tried to come in, but she stayed still floating, forcing herself breathe normally.

He was headed for their things and didn't seem to notice she hadn't started swimming yet.

*No one is watching me. He believes in me so much he's not even watching to see if I can do it. ... The salty water makes it easy to float here.* She eyed the Kon Tiki boat and slowly started to swim toward it.

# CHAPTER THIRTEEN

*K*ara swam in slow strokes toward the boat.

*This isn't so bad. If I had a place at home like this to swim in, I might learn to be less afraid and maybe even become a good swimmer.*

Even after she had taken the class for timid non-swimmers, she still had to fight the phobia. It hadn't cured her. She wasn't sure what would.

Kara reached the Kon Tiki boat and climbed aboard then glanced back at Nate and saw him watching her with a pleased smile as he carried her things.

She beamed back at him, feeling proud as she sat on a bench. Small grains of salt and sand covered her, and she wished they had a place to rinse off, but thrilled to have swum to the boat, the thought barely registered before Nate sat beside her.

"Sweetheart, you did great. I'm proud of you."

Kara beamed and he kissed her cheek.

"I didn't think you saw me."

"I was watching you the whole time. I saw you hesitating and then you faced your fears and swam right over to the boat." He'd seemed nonchalant as if he wasn't looking, but all the time he'd watched her, making sure she was okay. That knowledge warmed her even more than his arm wrapped around her.

He kissed her ear and it sent tingles down her spine. "Let's have dinner alone. Just the two of us."

"Can we do that? Have a table to ourselves?"

"Sweetheart, we can do whatever we want."

"Then yes. I'd like that."

"Good. I think we should celebrate."

"Oh? What are we celebrating?"

"A woman learning to conquer her fear."

She blushed, feeling proud all the same.

On the ride back, the crew covered the glass bottom and set up poles for the limbo contest. Kara clapped with the music as Nate, Adam and Viv all did the limbo. They couldn't convince her to join them. She'd done one daring thing today swimming to the boat and one was enough. She just wanted to bask in that for now.

Watching Nate's strong, sun-kissed body cross under the limbo poles, her heart beat more rapidly. She watched the muscles in his thighs and her heart drummed with the pulse of the music as the passengers sung, "How low can you go, go, go."

Other women watched him with appreciation. But he only watched Kara.

A warm glow rippled through her.

Nate made her feel alive, attractive and desirable. And braver. Already she'd tried things she'd never done before. She had Nate to thank for that.

She hated the thought that the cruise would end and she'd never see him again. She pushed away the thought as she watched Viv do the limbo next. Short and feisty, Viv bounced as she went beneath the bar.

*I don't want to be like Viv, moving from one man to another like it's no big thing. I give my heart too deeply to recover and move on to the next guy. I just can't do casual sex. That's not for me. And Viv is wrong. All men are not the same. Just as there'd never be another Neil, there will never be another Nate.*

*And I think he is the one.*

*No, I know he is.*

*One night with him before this cruise is over, that's all I wish for, one wonderful night to remember for the rest of my life. To say goodbye and never to have made love, I think I would die a very slow death. A death of the heart and soul.*

The thought brought a tear to her eye, which then tried to roll down her cheek before she brushed it away and forced a smile back onto her face.

How had she gone from elation to tears? Goodness, she had to get a grip on herself instead of letting her emotions take over.

The contest was finished and Viv had won because she was so much smaller than the others. She wore a triumphant smirk and everyone congratulated her.

The boat had been moving along and they were soon back at the pier ready to disembark.

Nate cupped her chin in his hand. His touch was almost unbearable in its tenderness. In the back of her mind, the clock ticked away and reminded her their time together would soon run out.

"Well, sweetheart, time to go clean up for our private dinner. I'll call you once the arrangements are made."

He bent and kissed her in front of the passengers who hadn't disembarked yet. His kiss was tender and light as a summer breeze.

"I'll see you at dinner." The look on his face mingled eagerness and tenderness.

A burning desire, an aching need for another kiss and more than a kiss coursed through Kara. "Yes, I'll see you at dinner," she echoed.

They parted and Kara went to get ready. Tonight's theme was Island Night, and there'd be an island deck party later on. She chose to wear the new yellow sundress and banana earrings.

Viv was still primping when Kara left for dinner.

*It was nice not to have to wait on Viv.* Tonight

they'd barely said two words to each other beyond Viv's comment that Kara looked like a banana in yellow. A comment Kara ignored. She was ignoring a lot lately. Viv's moods and comments grated on Kara's nerves.

Nate waited for her at the entrance to the private dining room. His look caressed her shoulders, and she sheepishly said, "I got a bit too much sun again today."

His smile curled her toes. "Take care of your skin, sweetheart. It's too beautiful to ruin."

The admiration in his eyes heated her cheeks beneath her already heated skin.

"You look so fresh and pretty in that dress, sweetheart."

"Yellow is my favorite color. It's cheerful."

"It goes with your golden hair."

"Viv called me a banana."

"She's crazy. You look great."

"Thank you. I've never owned a yellow dress before."

"Terrible." He shook his head and smiled.

"That's why I treated myself."

"As you should. You remind me of an exotic tropical bird." He winked. "Yes, I think I'll call you yellow bird." His whole face lit with a smile.

Kara giggled. He made her giddy as a schoolgirl. "Yellow bird." She returned his smile. "I like that."

The host seated them at a private table for two

off in a quiet corner. They ordered, sipped fine wine, and took turns feeding each other shrimp cocktail, lobster tail and crab legs. Kara had never had such an intimate meal before and anticipated each delicious morsel he fed her.

They decided to share dessert. Their waiter brought out a large slice of chocolate cake drizzled with caramel and two forks.

Kara liked sharing desert.

There was something about the way a man ate, the way a man shared or didn't share his food, which suggested what kind of lover he'd be. Though she'd known only two men intimately, something told her this was a truth. She watched Nate savor his food, and it reminded her of how he seemed to savor her body.

"You can have the last bite, sweetheart." He slipped it onto his fork and held it out to her.

*He'd be considerate and generous to his wife, and she'd know she's well loved. It doesn't do to think about the future with a man I've just met. It doesn't do to think of growing old together in some fantasy happy ever after land when you know you could never be with the man you loved. When you knew he would leave.*

Why was she thinking such thoughts when the most she could hope to have was one night together, one special memory to hold onto? Kara pushed all those thoughts away.

After dinner they went up on deck, where everything was decorated for a tropical evening. The waiters wore leis and tropical print shirts.

The activities director stood ready to teach a native dance to the passengers.

"Go on," Nate said. "I'll enjoy watching you."

She joined the dancers. Nate's gaze upon her made her feel exotic, like a tropical bird, rare and valuable. She danced only for him, blushing and rolling her hips. His smile deepened.

The conga line around the room was the grand finale. Nate stepped behind Kara and whispered in her ear, "I'm right behind you, sweetheart."

His warm hands slid around her hips and rested there lightly, her body tingling from the contact. She wished he'd pull her back against his chest so she could feel his arms around her. She hungered from the memory of his mouth, his touch.

The dance stopped and his hands dropped from her hips. She turned to face him. "Are you looking forward to the show?"

"I'm looking forward to the entire evening," he said, his hand closing over hers. "Sweetheart, I'm just happy we're spending it together."

Kara couldn't remember when she'd felt so happy. It was almost a giddiness within that made her want to spin about the room and laugh. She had been ready to be bold like Viv and suggest they find one of their empty cabins, and he was just happy to be spending time with her. Within her must live a wild and wanton thing. She was a little afraid of that, so she made the decision to follow along where he might lead. The child in her really did want to see the show. Chinese acrobats that she'd heard were fabulous.

They headed to the main stage show. Nate slid into the seat next to her and closed his hand over hers, turning it over. His finger caressed her palm in slow circles and she remained motionless, a warming shiver moving through her.

*Breathe. Remember to breathe.*

Her skin tingled as he touched her, and the urgent hum built. She glanced at his profile as he watched the show. The beginning of a smile tipped the corners of his mouth. He turned toward her and amusement flickered in his eyes.

"You're going to miss the show," he said in a light, teasing way as his finger continued making a circular pattern.

Kara blushed at her own excitement, glad the semidarkness hid the flush in her cheeks. She turned back to watch the show and tried to ignore the strange ache in her heart. The ache made her want to capture each moment and hold it, along with the knowledge they had so little time. Every moment was precious.

Through the entire show, she half-watched half-dreamed of what his touch could do, was doing. The anticipation of what would happen later hovered in her mind.

The show ended, Nate released her hand, and she tried to get her breath under control.

*What is it about him that sends my senses spinning?* The slightest touch and she wanted to fall into his arms.

They moved through the crowd and toward the exit, Nate placing his fingertips against the small of her back. Warmth spread through her body like an explosive current.

"I've got you, yellow bird." His breath ruffled her hair. The crowd pushed closer. His hands settled around her waist, guiding her in front of him, pulling her back out of the way of a large, drunk man who stumbled in front of her.

Kara felt treasured. If only she'd relax and stop thinking, but they only had two more days together.

When they reached the poolside deck again, waiters handed out brightly colored leis. Nate draped a red lei over her head before slipping on his own. Couples danced on the deck in front of the band, and Nate pulled her to the front of the stage.

"Wait here, sweetheart," he said.

"All right," she replied, puzzled he'd lead her to the dance floor and expect her to stand waiting. He stepped close to the drummer to speak to him. The man nodded, and Nate returned to gather her in his arms.

They swayed together until the song ended. Nate grinned as the bandleader dedicated the next song to Kara and the band played "Yellow Bird."

Nate sang softly, "Yellow bird, up high in banana tree. Yellow bird, you sit all alone like me."

His husky voice sent tingles down her spine. She'd never had a man sing to her until tonight. Neil couldn't carry a tune.

His eyes looked down into hers with intensity.

"Wish that I were a yellow bird, I'd fly away with you," he sang and pulled her closer.

*I wish we could fly away, too.*

She closed her eyes, and then the song ended. The band switched to another melody.

"Your skin almost matches this red lei," he said. Lifting one hand, he slipped his fingers under the strap of her yellow dress and lightly grazed her shoulder with a whisper of a touch.

"Does it hurt?"

"Only a little."

His fingers slid slowly down her bare arm, a brief caress.

"You're warm."

*That was an understatement.*

Nate eased his arm around her back and they moved across the floor in a waltz. It was too easy to get lost in the way he looked at her. She closed her eyes. Ocean breezes blew across her heated skin.

He whispered in her ear, "You look beautiful tonight, yellow bird."

She giggled.

Warmth spread through her body at his words and the way his hand moved up and down the small of her back pulling her closer. He smelled so good, like spices and salty seas. She put her arms around his neck. The longing to be held nearly overwhelmed her.

He danced her away from the other couples. He kissed her earlobe and tingles spread down her spine all the way to her toes.

He released her to look into her eyes then leaned forward and kissed her lips, gentle at first until she parted them.

They stood swaying to the music, locked in a lovers embrace. His tongue slipped inside her mouth, exploring. Her breath quickened as the tip of his tongue met hers in another kind of dance. His heart thudded beneath her palm. She no longer knew if the music had changed and was aware of nothing beyond the two of them.

He cupped her face in his hands and deepened the kiss.

NATE COULDN'T GET ENOUGH of Kara. He loved the way she tasted, her scent, the softness of her skin and hair. He loved the sound of her laugh, her giggle.

He didn't want to let her go and wished the cruise lasted longer, that they had more time together.

But more than the physical attraction, more than that pull, he cared about her, wanted to see her happy and wanted to remain in her life, whatever it took.

He wanted to take it slow, though the heat building between them made it harder and harder. Had she been a different women he'd have taken her off to bed already. But spending time with Kara, the woman who made his heart soar, brought him happiness beyond the strong physical attraction that pulled him to her .

# CHAPTER FOURTEEN

Kara was so swept away by the way Nate kissed her that when he stopped it took her a moment to realize where they were and that there were other people around.

Gazing into his eyes, the realization dawned that he pulled back from taking things further. Her heart sank.

She turned and walked over to the side of the ship and stood gazing out at the water.

"Kara, what's wrong?" He'd followed her and now reached for her hand. "Tell me, sweetheart."

She turned to face him, not shielding or wiping away the tears that gathered in her eyes. "We have so little time." One tear escaped and rolled down her cheek as her voice dropped to a whisper. "And I don't want to go back to my cabin and sleep alone again tonight."

Surprise came across his face. He pulled her to him and wrapped his arms around her. "Sweetheart, are you ready for that? You're sure?"

"Yes, yes," she said impatiently. "Please carry me off to your cabin as soon as possible."

He threw his head back and laughed. "You want me to carry you?"

She smiled. "Well it's just an expression..." Her words trailed off as he lifted her up into his arms. "Oh! Oh my."

She wrapped her arms around his neck, and he carried her down below decks, through hallways with her giggling, giddy as a schoolgirl.

When they reached his stateroom he put her down and opened the door for her. "After you."

She stepped inside and looked around.

The cabin was larger than the one she and Viv shared and had sliding glass doors and a balcony. "Oh, this is nice."

"Yes, it is. Perks of my travel agent cousin." He walked over to the doors and slid them open.

A breeze stirred the white curtains as she walked nearer.

"Come out with me." He stepped out onto the balcony.

Kara joined him. It was windy but he pulled her close to keep her warm.

They stood silently watching the sea and then he

moved behind her, lifted her hair, and kissed the back of her neck. As he landed kiss after kiss upon her skin, tiny goose bumps rose from the way his lips felt against her heated skin. He moved in front of her and kissed her lips, his hands sliding across her body, from her hips up her rib cage to cup her breasts as he deepened the kiss.

She longed to be free of her clothing, of anything between them and impatience caused her to break off from the kiss.

He watched her, reading her expression, so she gave him what she thought was a sultry smile and slid one strap of her dress off one shoulder and then the other.

His eyes darkened with desire as he watched her.

She let the dress fall to the floor and stood only in white lace panties as the moon came out from behind the clouds bathing her in its light.

His gaze took her in. "Beautiful."

Beneath his gaze and the light of the moon, she felt beautiful.

Her took her hand, lifted it to his lips, turning it to kiss the inside of her wrist, moving closer with each kiss he rained from her wrist to her elbow. Threading his fingers through hers he led her toward the door. She followed wearing nothing but her panties and heels, the dress forgotten on the floor.

Inside the door, he scooped her up in his arms again and laid her on the bed. Giving her a soft kiss on the lips, he stood. "Stay," he said. "I'll be right back."

He strode into the bathroom and returned wearing nothing but boxer shorts and carrying a bottle of lotion. He placed it on the table and reached to lift her heel.

His warm hand wrapped around her ankle. He slipped the heel strap of her sandal off slowly. Then he tossed it over his shoulder.

She giggled.

He bent and kissed the sole of her foot, still holding her ankle, before kissing from the sole of her foot all along the inside of her leg to her knee, watching her all the while, reading the way she reacted to his touch and his kiss, every breath, the way her body warmed, as she felt herself melting into the bed. He did the same with the other foot until he reached her other knee.

He stopped only to breathe one word across her skin. "Beautiful."

She had never felt so adored, so treasured in her life.

Expecting him to continue on to remove her panties or to move up to her breasts, he surprised her when he said, "Roll over."

She did, but a sense of disappointment came over her.

Would their first time not be face to face?

She missed the intimacy of looking into his eyes and wondered what he was thinking, what he would do next. When she turned to look at him, he said, "Lie still. I'll put some aloe vera lotion on that sunburn."

He moved her hair to one side over her shoulder and she expected him to kiss her neck or shoulder.

Instead she felt cool lotion between his warm hand and her over-heated skin, where the sun had kissed her a bit too much. He smoothed cooling aloe vera lotion into her back and it soothed her skin, her mind and her soul. Her eyes drifted closed.

A few moments later, he shifted then rolled her over to look at him. "Better?"

"Yes. Thank you."

"My pleasure."

There was a pause as they looked into each other's eyes, both smiling. Then he began to trace his finger across her collarbone, before bending to kiss her there, the kisses again showering down her body, slow and steady.

She floated in a sea of bliss as the movements of the ship sailing at night and Nate's caresses and kisses swept her away. She lost track of what he did when, closed her eyes and gave herself over to him, her fingers clutching the sheets, her body arching, until wave after wave came over her and she cried out.

Like the sea their night together was one wave after another crashing upon the beach they shared. She lost track of how many waves there were, how many small ones lead up to the largest one. How many small broken pieces of herself were swept away beneath his loving touch, his whispered words.

And when the sun rose and they gazed into each other's eyes, she knew she'd received so much more than her wish for one night with him, for there would never be another night in all her life like this one.

KARA LET herself into her cabin and undressed before climbing into bed, careful not to wake Viv, who kept up a steady snore. It had been so hard to leave Nate. He asked her to stay. But it was easier like this, with nothing to mar the memories of the night they'd spent and no tears to stain his sheets or chest. She left amid a haze of happiness. The tears would come later, but in this happy state she could keep them at bay for a little while.

It seemed she'd just gone to sleep when Viv woke her with a shake of her shoulder.

"You awake, Kara?"

Kara moaned. "I am now." She opened one bleary eye. "What do you want?"

"I've gotta tell you about the guy walking in on Adam and me last night."

"What guy?"

"Oh, you know. The room steward, what's his name?"

Kara couldn't think of it either. At the moment she didn't care.

"Anyway, our room steward must have thought the room was empty. We'd been in and out of it. We can't keep our hands off each other. That man is so fine. Okay, so we'd gone up to have a drink at the bar and ended up back here fifteen minutes later and the guy must have thought we'd be out longer. Adam and I had stripped and were starting to have it away when he walked in."

*She woke me up for this?*

Kara groaned and pulled the covers up over her head.

Viv pulled them back and peered at her. "What's the matter? You have a hangover? Need aspirin?"

"No, I don't have a hangover. What I need is sleep. And it serves you right for forgetting the 'do not disturb' sign."

"Oh, I'm not upset about that! It was actually funny. It's what happened after."

Kara sighed. "What happened?"

"I joked that the guy could join us, but Adam got mad and said he wasn't into that."

"Gee, I can't imagine why."

"No, seriously. The man must be half in love with me already and that's why he got mad. So we've had our first fight. Can you believe he told me I was too hot for him?" She sank onto the bed with a look of amazement.

"You know, Viv, you may have finally found a guy who actually cares about you more than getting into your pants. There are good guys out there."

"I've never had a man tell me 'no' before. It's quite novel. Should I be insulted or flattered? He's so good looking and sexy as hell when he's in the mood."

"Viv, you're like an alley cat. If you were a man, women would run from you."

"Hey now."

"I mean it. Look, you've met a nice guy for once. Maybe one who has some morals and might treat you right? And you think there's something wrong with him? Have you ever thought he might respect you?"

"No." Viv frowned. "What do you know about men anyhow?"

*I know I have more respect for myself than you do. I know I deserve to be treated right.*

*Maybe it's Viv who needs advice about men.*

"I may not be as experienced at dating as you are, but I know what I want and how I want to be treated. And I'm guessing deep down you do too."

"Yeah, maybe." Viv shrugged. "He won't hang

with me today. He said he'd call. I hate it when they say that. I'll call you is the kiss of death. Because they don't." Viv looked dejected.

*Could Viv really care for Adam as more than a simple fling?*

"You can come with me, I'm getting my hair braided on Blissful Cay," Kara said.

"Ooh! Sounds like fun! I'll have mine done, too."

Islanders had offered to braid their hair on each island. Today the ship anchored just off Blissful Cay, the cruise line's private island.

"Yes, that'll be fun. I'll need a nap at some point though because I didn't get in till two."

"Oh!" Viv's eyes widened. "Tell me, tell me."

"Nate and I stayed up until two and it was wonderful."

"You got laid. Finally."

"I did not get laid. We spent a wonderful evening together, but it was not like that."

*It was so much more than that.* Memories of the gentle caring way he'd slowly made love to her filled her mind. *What we shared tonight was beautiful. I'm ruining it by talking about it to Viv.*

Viv frowned. "Well, if you didn't get laid, you're running out of time."

"I didn't get any sleep last night, if that answers your question. And you can now stop worrying about my sex life, okay? So drop it."

*I don't expect her to understand and she's just going*

*to get jealous if I say much more. What Nate and I shared is private and I'm not going to discuss it with her.*

"The tenders will be taking passengers back and forth every half hour." Kara yawned. "We have all day. So there's no hurry."

"Don't you want to get your hair braided before you see Nate again? You'll be sexy, like Bo Derek in that movie *Ten*."

*Well, that's an idea. I'm awake now anyway.*

Kara got up and they went to the café for coffee and pastries. For a while it was like old times back when they were in high school. They talked about hairstyles, movies and how the movie *Ten* had made the braiding style popular among white women.

They wore swimsuits beneath their cover-ups, carried beach bags loaded with supplies for the day, and headed for the tender station.

Kara eyed the ship's tender, a smaller boat that carried passengers to and from the shore. The ship bobbed by the side of the cruise ship, rocked by the sea. Crewmen stood by the ramp to help her in, but she still hesitated. The ship sat far from shore in deep water

"Come on, fraidy cat, you're holding up the line," Viv said.

Kara winced and stepped forward, embarrassed.

∾

KARA AND VIV boarded the boat tender.

Nate boarded and walked to where they sat. "Hello."

"Hello," they both chorused.

He turned to Kara. "I hope you slept well."

"Yes, quite well until Viv woke me up. And you?"

"Very well, thank you. I dreamed of a golden haired woman."

She blushed.

"Have fun shopping," he said. "I'll be playing volleyball if you want to find me later." He winked.

"Okay."

He moved to the front and stood looking out at the sea as they sailed toward shore.

Kara watched Nate standing with the wind in his hair. *It was evident how much he loved the sea.*

Watching him gave her pleasure and she smiled, seeing the contentment and ease with which he stood.

The tender docked, and the passengers exited. Kara and Viv headed to the hut where island women sat beading passenger's hair. They waited their turns, listening to the island women tell stories of silly things their men did while trying to woo them.

One man had brought a swordfish to her father when he asked for her hand in marriage. The second suitor had more money, and he brought several bottles of rum. She'd chosen the one with the swordfish over her father's objections.

"You want de man who can do tings," she said. "De man who can do, well, he do wit out de money. But de man wit de money dat cannot do, when dat money is gone den what he good for?"

"An' him drinkin' all dat rum all de time, too," her friend said.

Both women nodded and Kara and Viv laughed.

Viv sported a few little braids on each side of her face. It took much longer to braid Kara's long blonde hair, but she felt like an island queen when it was done. She turned her head from side to side as the beads swung.

"Very sexy," the woman said handing her a mirror.

Looking into it Kara gasped.

The hairdo brought out her cheekbones and eyes.

Viv watched in silence.

Kara smiled and gave the woman a big tip. "Thank you."

"Men don't want no skinny girl. You have de woman's hips," the woman said. "Good for makin' dem babies."

Maybe. But she'd no luck "makin' babies" with Neil. That had never bothered him as it had her.

Kara and Viv shopped, admiring the straw dolls, purses, and dark woodcarvings. They found hammocks in the shade and Kara put her bag down next to the palm tree hers was tied to.

"Viv?"

Viv had stopped with her mouth hanging open.

Kara glanced in the direction of Viv's gaze. Adam was spreading lotion over a petite blonde's back.

"Well, he's not wasting any time." Anger radiated off her.

"Oh no. Sorry, Viv."

*Wow, she's really fallen for him. I've never seen her this disappointed before.*

"See, Kara. They're all the same. Even the so-called good ones." Viv stood with her fists on her hips. She tossed her head. "Right-o. Watch this. And keep an eye on my stuff."

Viv jogged over to the men lining up for volleyball. She stripped off her swimsuit cover-up and tossed it into the sand. A muscle-bound guy whistled at the sight of Viv in her bikini. *That was Viv, back in the game.* One more woman joined and they started to play.

Adam finished rubbing the blonde's back and stood. He glanced over to the volleyball game where the men all watched Viv bounce around on the sand. In her bikini top, Viv had some bounce going and she'd play it up.

*Where was Nate?* Kara glanced around but didn't see him.

She climbed into the hammock and lay back, closing her eyes. Viv would wake her when the game was over.

~

NATE SPOTTED Kara's red bikini then carried his snorkel gear over to where she seemed to be sleeping. He had no trouble finding her since she wore the sexy red bikini again. She had had her hair braided.

He reached out and touched one of her braids. "Looks nice, sweetheart. How's it feel?"

She opened her eyes and looked at him. "Hello."

"Hello, yellow bird." He smiled.

"It feels different. But I like it. And I can leave it in for a week without having to do my hair. No more tangles."

He toyed with her braids. "You're beautiful in this or any other hairstyle."

The memory of the previous evening and his murmured use of the word as he had made love to her caused her to flush. "Thank you."

"It's true. Bought you something." He held out a bag.

"Oh," she sat up and reached for the bag, thrilled that he had bought her a present. "Thank you."

Inside the bag was a straw purse made by the island ladies with a yellow bird on the front.

"It made me think of you."

She gave a joyful laugh. "I love it. It's perfect. Thank you."

"My pleasure, sweetheart."

He lifted the snorkel gear. "I thought you might like to try snorkeling again."

"But I'd have had to rent a set."

"No, I brought two, mine and Adam's."

"I didn't know you brought your own."

"I usually go out on my own, not on tours, unless I'm running them."

"It's probably better to have your own gear."

"It is. So, how about it?"

Kara glanced at the water, a sense of alarm coming over her again at how deep and strong the ocean was.

"We'll snorkel over there." He gestured further down the beach to a wooden platform with steps jutting out into the water. Adults and children were lined up on the platform. "I know you're still learning."

"Okay, I'll try it again."

They walked down the beach to the platform but when they got in line, she looked up at him in alarm. "I can't swim without a vest. I can't put my head under if I'm not wearing one. I'm sorry, Nate, I, I can't do this."

"Sweetheart, calm down." He put his hand on her shoulder. "I'll rent you one."

"Oh, I don't want you to have to do that."

"Too late." He set down the gear and took off at a jog over to the rental hut.

She stood by the gear feeling like a big baby. He'd

never seen her in full-blown panic. Maybe he wouldn't be as attracted to her then. Maybe he'd want to wash his hands of her.

*He was a man who went scuba diving for God's sake. What was he doing with her and not some scuba diving female?*

Soon he returned with a yellow snorkel vest that looked like a bib. She glanced at it doubtfully. Last time they'd snorkeled she'd worn a full ski vest.

"This is all you need sweetheart." He grinned. "It will hold you up." He took the ski vest, put his mouth to it and began to inflate it.

*Great. Nothing like floating in the ocean, wearing a balloon for floatation.*

Nate walked down the steps into the water first. Then he swam nearby and waited for her as she made her way down the steps carrying her flippers and goggles.

She struggled trying to put all the gear on as frustration and fear churned her stomach.

"Here, sweetheart." He took her mask. "Take your time and try putting your flippers on first."

She slipped her feet into the flippers, but they were too big because they were men's and she had to scrunch her toes to keep them on.

"Okay, now your mask." He adjusted the strap to fit her then eased it over her braids. "Comfortable?"

She shook her head. "No."

He fiddled with the strap a moment. "There. Better?"

"Yes."

"Good." He smiled then put his goggles and mouthpiece on and his head down into the water.

Kara swam alongside him, but the flippers were awkward and the little snorkel vest seemed flimsy. How would she ever get her nerve to put her head in?

After a minute, he popped his head up and took out his mouthpiece. "What's wrong, sweetheart'?"

"I..." She was embarrassed to tell him.

Nate's gaze was tender and understanding. He held out his hand. "Relax. You can do this."

She placed her hand in his. "Okay, but go slow."

"Slow as you want, sweetheart."

The strength in his hand captured her fear and held it until her own strength found a hold. They swam leaning down into the water, moving out to where the fish were plentiful.

Kara beheld the magnificent world below, her eyes wide with wonder and she glanced at Nate. He looked back into her eyes communicating in silence. His gaze flicked away as a movement caught his eye, and he squeezed her hand quickly then pointed down.

A cannon rested beneath them on the sand. Small fish wove in and out below the wheels. A bright blue fish darted out of the mouth of the cannon, then as if it had seen them watching, darted right back in. She glanced at Nate, and he winked and pointed her farther out to sea.

She wasn't afraid with him there, holding her hand. She would have followed him anywhere.

She nodded and allowed him to lead her to a sunken statue of a woman. Plant life had grown up around her and the coral waved in slow motion. A large, green plant looking like green cauliflower jutted out of the white rocks, and small yellow and black striped fish swam around it. Green seaweed also waved slowly, like everything else in this underwater world.

*Was this what it was like to be deaf? To view everything around you like a silent movie?*

Without sound, the slightest movement in her peripheral vision caught her attention.

*Did the deaf see life like this? Did colors appear more vivid? Did they notice movement more quickly?*

Small fish fled as if afraid of something large.

*Shark? Oh God.*

She couldn't breathe. Her heart raced and she felt lightheaded.

*How far out to sea? Air. Oh God.*

Nate was turned away, pointing at something. She squeezed his hand and popped her head out of the water, pulling off her mask and snorkel, gasping.

Nate lifted his head past the surface and

removed his mouthpiece. "Kara, sweetheart; what's wrong?"

She felt clammy and sweat had broken out on her forehead, even though they were in the water. She gasped and reached for him. "Shark."

"Where?"

She pointed.

He pulled on his gear and put his head under to look then popped back up again. "No sharks."

"The fish were running away." Her voice shook.

He pulled her close, wrapping one arm around her, his eyes dark with emotion. "Kara," the warmth in his voice chided her, "it was just a big fish. No sharks. Why are you so afraid? Do you honestly think I'd let anything happen to you?"

"No. But the fish ran."

Featherlike laugh lines crinkled around his eyes as he smiled. "They just startle easy. Think how we must look to them. And we are predators because we might eat them."

She gave a nervous laugh and gazed out to sea. The horizon appeared vast and flat from where they floated. "Would we even see a shark before it was too late?"

Nate pulled her close until they were almost nose-to-nose. "Do you have any idea how rare shark attacks are?"

She shook her head, now studying crinkles in the corners of his eyes. He was a man who'd age well.

She liked his smile lines and she could get lost in his deep brown eyes.

"You're more likely to be killed in a car accident than any other kind yet you still drive, right?"

"Yes. Every day."

"This is no different." He watched her, silent for a moment. "Sweetheart you worry too much."

But worry had become a part of her, and she couldn't stop the thoughts forcing their way in.

*If we stayed together, he'd be frustrated with me eventually when the newness wears off. I'm not his perfect mate. What is he doing with a woman who's afraid of water? He isn't afraid of anything. And he loves the water. He won't understand. How can he understand this? Once he realizes my phobia isn't going away, it will be over between us. Swim lesson for fraidy cats didn't cure me. Nothing will.*

He drew her against his chest and kissed her. Every thought and worry flew from her like he'd let loose a flock of birds. When he released her, her breath caught in her throat and she felt her heart pounding.

"You have to stop worrying so much." His grin sent warmth straight down to her toes. "You'll worry yourself to death." He kissed her again. "Let me take your mind off of your worries."

His arms held her firmly as his lips directed her thoughts away from everything but the warmth and strength of his touch. When he finally released her, her legs felt like they'd turned into jellyfish.

Kara floated next to him, letting the water bob her up and down, and tried to catch her breath. With him next to her, she felt as if she could do anything. An awakened sense of life excited her. Could she keep that feeling once he'd gone? Would her newly found courage vanish without him and her fears crowd in again?

# CHAPTER FIFTEEN

"*L*et's get some lunch," Nate said. "Smell that barbeque?"

Kara glanced toward the beach where the lunch line stretched beyond the grass covered picnic area. Her mouth watered. "Oh, that does smell good. I didn't realize I was so hungry."

They swam back to the dock, then she handed him her gear and he helped her up the steps. As they dropped the rented snorkel gear off she realized he'd selected a yellow vest for her. He'd remembered it was her favorite color.

They joined the lunch line; his forefinger linked around her little finger with a light touch as they moved forward.

*How good to feel like a couple again.* It was little things like this; nonverbal things she had missed. She had missed sex. *It had been far to long.* But this,

this loving companionship fed Kara's soul. She wanted it, needed it and without it, she sat sad and alone in her cold empty house in Ohio. Lonely and longing to find a loving companion.

He released her finger so they could carry their plates. She smiled as she watched him move through the line, heaping his plate with potato salad and barbequed chicken. "You're hungry."

"You worked up my appetite, sweetheart. More than you know."

His voice rumbled through her body as if he had plucked a string within her.

*He meant more than one kind of hunger.* The fire from the barbeque pit now seemed warm.

Viv stood and waved them over.

"How was the snorkeling?" Adam asked.

"Fun," Kara said.

*So Viv and Adam had patched things up. That didn't take long.*

Nate glanced at her over the chicken wing he was eating. He didn't say a word about what a scaredy cat she was, and she realized he never would.

He licked the corner of his mouth, where a dab of barbeque sauce remained. Must his every movement remind her of his kiss, his touch, and his tongue? Her eyes roamed over his face. She might never see him again once this cruise was over. The thought made her want to memorize every single detail of his face.

Nate pushed his plate back and stood. "Dessert?"

"If you'll share one with me."

"Love to, sweetheart. What would you like?"

"Surprise me." She smiled.

He returned with a dish of vanilla ice cream and two spoons, sat and offered her a spoon along with that irresistible grin. She reached for the spoon and then took a bite, closing her eyes, savoring the cool sweetness.

"Good?"

She opened her eyes to find him watching her, his eyes shining with boyish charm. "Yes, very good."

They watched each other without speaking, eating the ice cream bite by bite, the only language between them their eyes and smiles.

When they finished he held up the bowl. "More?"

"No. I'm full."

He rubbed his hand over his washboard stomach. "I'm pleasantly full myself. Ready for a nap."

"Are you going back to the ship?"

"No. I thought we might find a hammock to share. Neither of us got enough sleep last night."

"Together? In the same hammock?"

"Sure. They can hold both of us."

How she'd sleep in a hammock next to him, she didn't know. Not the way her body would cry out for him to touch her.

The hammock hung beneath two palm trees, a quiet shady spot with a breeze.

His finger traced her jaw line then he caressed her neck, slowly brushing across her carotid artery. His eyes told her he'd felt the leap in her pulse and knew his affect on her. Dropping his hands, he bent and placed a soft kiss upon her lips before stepping back.

"I'm ready for a nap," he said. He moved to the hammock and sat, kicked off his sandals, then laid back and closed his eyes.

She stood speechless, watching the hammock swing with him in it. Eyes closed, he looked as though he hadn't a care in the world. As if he was completely unaffected by the intimacy of touching her skin, kissing her lips.

Oh, how she longed for him to kiss her again.

It wasn't possible she'd nap, but she climbed in beside him and his arm curled around her, pulling her close. He simply held her and despite what she'd thought, it was so comforting being in his arms, her head on his shoulder, that she drifted right off to sleep.

"Kara, wake up."

She reluctantly woke from a dream of Nate kissing her. Confused she opened her eyes and looked at Nate.

"We've slept too late. We'll miss the last tender if we don't hurry."

Flustered, she got up and slipped on her sandals. "Won't the ship wait for us?"

"No, it won't. Much as I'd love to be marooned on a private island with you," he smiled, his gaze caressing her heated skin. "We need to get you out of this sun."

Her sunburn had gotten worse even though she'd put sun block on.

"Come on. We'll have to run." He reached for her hand, grasped it, and they ran together down to the pier to the last tender, making it just in time before it left.

They jumped onto the boat, and then Kara realized she'd just jumped into the same boat she'd been afraid to step into earlier. With Nate beside her, she'd felt no fear.

When the tender pulled up to the side of the cruise ship, she felt brave enough to climb out by herself without help. He smiled encouragement. They parted company at the elevator to go get ready for dinner.

When Kara opened the door to the stateroom, Viv who'd been pacing rushed over. "Oh my God, Kara. I was so worried!"

"Worried?"

"Yes, worried. When they called your name over the loudspeaker to report to the ship's desk I thought something terrible had happened. Our room steward said they call the names of passengers who haven't made it back, but the ship sails whether you're on it or not. They don't wait for anyone."

"Oh, God, Viv. Sorry to have worried you. I'll call the front desk to let them know I'm here." She made the call then turned back to Viv.

"So, were you trying to stow away on the island or were you so into each other you lost track of time?"

"No." Kara said, exasperated. "We just fell asleep."

"He looks like a man who could wear a woman out."

Kara rolled her eyes. "We took an innocent nap."

"Nate is anything but innocent. This isn't some fairy tale happy ever after. Trust me on this one. That man could have any woman he wanted on this ship, and he wants you. But there's nothing innocent about it. He wants you in his bed and just wants to have a good time. Don't make him into some romantic hero he isn't."

*What is wrong with her? Is she jealous? Nate isn't like that, but I'm not discussing him with her.*

"I don't want to talk about it. I'm getting a shower."

"Well, I told Adam we'd meet them for cocktails before dinner, so hurry."

*Oh, she did not just tell me to hurry. After waiting on her again and again while she primps?*

"No, Viv, what I need is a good long shower to get the sand out of my braids. I'll need some time in there. Go on without me."

Viv's jaw dropped open. Speechless, she stared at Kara.

"Kara, what is with you? It's not like you to almost miss the ship. I can't believe you did that. This behavior is so unlike you. What were you thinking?"

"Sorry, Viv."

"I can't believe Adam and I wasted our time worrying and searching for the two of you. This cruise is almost over. Adam and I could've been doing something fun."

"I can't keep up with all your boyfriends. First you're going with that British guy, then you're with Adam and then you're not. When we got off on the private island, you were done with him. You two sure made up fast. But excuse me for wasting *your* time. Heaven forbid you miss out on some fun."

For the second time Viv stared at her without speaking.

Kara was too angry to say what she most wanted to say. *You're behaving like a selfish bitch.* Instead she stood silently, scowling at Viv as her thoughts churned. *This cruise sure has turned out to be all about you. Your fun, your time. You wouldn't even be on this cruise if not for me and you haven't had to pay a dime for it. But is there even an ounce of gratitude? Even so much as a simple thank you? No. Some friend. Some gratitude.*

"I don't know what's got your panties in such a

twist." Viv crossed her arms. "You're the one who kept everyone waiting."

*I've apologized for that once already. I'm not doing it again.*

"Go meet Adam for drinks." Kara ground out the words. "I'll see you at dinner."

"Fine." Viv grabbed her room key off the dresser and stormed out the door, slamming it.

*Well, good. She's gone and I have the cabin all to myself.*

She and Viv needed some space and this tiny cabin wasn't helping.

Kara glanced about the cabin where her room-mate's clothes and shoes were strewn. Viv had become even sloppier when she found out their cabin steward would pick everything up for her, putting shoes in the closet and folding or hanging up clothes when the room was straightened.

Kara was glad the theme tonight was country western because she didn't have to dress up. The shower felt wonderful and she had the tiny state-room to herself. Jeans, tee shirt, and a bandana around her neck and she was ready. She looked forward to dancing with Nate and she'd have a good time and forget about Viv.

She found the three of them waiting in line to be seated. Adam and Nate looked handsome in cowboy boots and hats. Nate wore a blue shirt that accentu-ated his tan and made Kara want to pop the buttons so she could run her fingers across his muscular chest.

"This is what took you so long?" Viv eyed Kara's jeans, white tee shirt that said Coca-cola, and the blue bandana around her neck. "I thought we might need to have them call for you again. In case you missed the boat."

Kara colored but retorted. "That isn't necessary."

And with that, Viv shut up and went back to drinking her appletini.

NATE DECIDED Kara looked just as good in blue jeans as she did in a dress. *Hell, she looks good in anything or nothing at all. Everything about her is beautiful.*

He was admiring Kara when Viv started in with her little comments. Nate had never cared for the way she spoke to Kara. As if she was somehow better than Kara. Not for the first time he wondered why Kara put up with it.

Tonight though, Kara seemed snappish with her best friend. It wasn't what she'd said, but more the tone she used. Something was bothering Kara.

*Obviously the women aren't getting along well.*

He took Kara's hand and pulled her a couple feet away from Viv and Adam. Brushing strands of hair behind her ear and looking down into her eyes he said, "We could skip the fancy dining tonight, if you want. The dinner buffet is open. It will be quieter and we can talk."

"Yes, let's," Kara said. "I'd like that."

He told Adam they had changed plans and were going off for a private meal. Adam nodded and Viv didn't say a word.

The dinner buffet had a full spread of food from prime rib to southern fried chicken to sushi or Chinese. Kara perked up once she was away from Viv.

"This food looks just as good as anything we've had in the main dining room."

"Possibly better. Not everything needs to have a special sauce," Nate said.

She laughed. "You're right. I've actually been craving fried chicken and mashed potatoes and gravy."

*Comfort food. Something is bothering her.*

"Well then, I'm glad they're serving that tonight." He smiled. "I saw a quiet table by the windows in the back corner." He nodded toward the window.

That section of the dining area stood empty and they headed for a table. Kara took her seat with a relieved sigh. "I'm glad you suggested this instead."

"It, uh, looked like you could use a break from Viv. And I admit I had an ulterior motive." He winked and leaned forward as if to share a secret. "I wanted you all to myself this evening." He wiggled his eyebrows.

Kara giggled. Drama free was what she needed. "These cabins are so small and Viv and I need a break from each other. It seems like every time we're in that cabin we start fighting. We never used to fight like this."

He watched her toy with her food. She caught herself doing it and stopped.

"You want to talk about it?"

She nodded. "I don't know why she's behaving the way she is, but she's not the Viv I used to know."

"People change."

"Yes, but she was my best friend and we were so close. I didn't notice anything different until I came to see her."

"How long had it been since you saw her?"

"At least a year."

"Lots of things can happen in a year."

"Well, she hasn't had anything traumatic happen. She found a good job and a nice apartment. Has a new car, new furniture, and new clothes. She doesn't even look the same. It's, it's like the old Viv is just gone."

"Maybe when she moved she decided to reinvent herself."

"I liked the old Viv better. She was my best friend."

Kara could tell by the look on his face there was something he wanted to say, but was holding back. "What are you thinking?"

"I'm not sure I should tell you. As you said, she's your best friend."

"No, I want to know what you think. You've been around her nearly as much as I have this week."

"Well, you may not have noticed this, but she's jealous."

"Jealous? Of me?"

He nodded. "That's probably the root of the problem. You're beautiful, intelligent, thoughtful, and loving."

Kara knew there was more than a grain of truth in what he said about Viv's jealousy. *It would ruin their friendship.* She nodded. "I think you may be right."

"If she's not feeling good about herself, she may try to pull you down in order to feel better. But sweetheart, don't let her do that to you. Stand up for yourself."

"I will."

"Good." He held out an egg roll. "Try a bite?"

"Yes, I love Chinese food." She took a small bite and smiled at him. He returned her smile and continued eating.

After they finished eating, they headed to the dance club, which was playing country western music. She followed Nate onto the dance floor, and they joined a line dance that had just started. He linked his thumbs into his back pockets and danced without a care.

Kara noticed how the other women eyed him. She wondered how many women he had back home. The music switched to a slow dance, and she moved into his arms feeling she belonged there.

They danced for a while. He sent her that sexy grin and her heart flipped. It felt dreamlike as he spun her around the room and the same floating feeling came over her that happened whenever he was near. He made her senses spin.

"Would you like to go up on deck?"

"Yes." That's not all she'd like.

He held out his hand. She slipped her hand in his, and they walked to the elevator then took it to the main outer deck. He led her to the rails, still holding her hand.

"The sky is clear tonight," he said.

The moon and stars were bright and they stopped to look up just in time to see a shooting star. Kara gasped and caught her breath as it fell.

"That was so beautiful," Kara whispered.

"Not near as beautiful as you, sweetheart." His voice rumbled in her ear.

He turned her to face him and his compelling eyes riveted her to the spot. He swept off his hat and then putting a large hand to her waist, he drew her closer and bent to kiss her.

His lips pressed against hers, gently covering her mouth, and she returned his kiss with reckless abandon, her arms moving around his back to hold onto him, pulling him closer, letting him know how much she wanted him.

Still his kiss deepened and she wanted to melt. His arm around her back held her close. He broke the kiss and gazed into her eyes, studying her with a curious intensity.

Delightful shivers of wanting ran through her.

"This is our last night at sea."

"I know." She answered, unable to keep the sadness out of her voice. Even though she'd wished with all her heart, after tonight she'd never see him again. Sorrow came over her and she drew a deep breath, forbidding herself to cry.

"I'd like to visit you, if that's all right," he said.

"Oh." A cry of relief escaped from her lips. She gazed up at him with longing and wonder as her heart soared. *It isn't the end. Wishes do come true. It isn't over.* "Yes," she said, "I'd like that."

He pulled a pen and paper out of his pocket. "Give me your address and phone number."

She gave them. He wrote them down and stuck them in his pocket. "We spent our first evening together standing by the deck, watching the waves."

She smiled. "I remember."

"Why don't we go have another cappuccino?"

She took the hand he offered her. "That sounds nice."

Kara's heart leapt. She wanted to dance and jump and shout.

*He wants to keep in touch. To see me again.*

Joy bubbled in her soul. Her emotions had taken a roller coaster ride and the sadness she'd felt only made her joy that much greater.

They entered the bar and sat, waiting for their drinks. Nate took her hand in his and rubbed his thumb across it in a slow soothing motion. "So, sweetheart, you'll be back to work on Monday."

"Yes, and I dread it."

"Because of the job or because of Daryl?"

"Both. I realized just before I came on this cruise it wasn't what I really wanted to be doing. That was before Daryl showed up. But I'm just not sure what I want to do instead."

"How are you going to handle Daryl?"

"I've told him we can only be friends. Since I only see him at work it should be okay. Awkward though. I need to find a new job and sell my house. There's a lot to do when I get home."

He looked so serious as he sat listening. "He's already stepped over the line. Showing up on the island. And he's probably the one who sent you those panties. You could charge him with sexual harassment right now."

"I was planning to leave the job anyway, but I don't even have a resume yet."

"You're my girlfriend and no one messes with my girlfriend. If he so much as touches you, threatens you, I'll kill him." The look in his eyes and the expression on his face told her he was serious. "If he gives you any trouble, any trouble at all, I want you to call me."

"I will."

"Good." He squeezed her hand. "If you get scared for any reason, or you just want to talk, call me."

"I will."

Just hearing him say these words made her feel safer.

*His girlfriend.* Her heart wanted to sing.

An announcement came and they were quiet, listening to directions for leaving their bags outside the rooms tonight.

"We have to go and pack." She sighed with regret. "We're out of time. I wish we had more time."

"I'll walk you back to your cabin. We have a little time yet. I pack fast." He winked.

He walked her back to her cabin and she turned to look up at him, knowing this would be their goodbye kiss.

As he bent down she rose up on her toes to reach him, her arms sliding around him as he pulled her close. Their lips met with a sweet harmony in a dance they'd done many times and knew well.

His kiss was slow, thoughtful, his tongue exploring the recesses of her mouth. She kissed him back, lingering, savoring each moment, and not wanting it to end. And yet there was a barely contained hunger within each of them that demanded more.

Raising his mouth from hers, he gazed into her eyes. They stood in silence, drinking each other up.

He touched his fingertip to her lips. "Good night, sweetheart."

"Good night, Nate." With reluctance she opened her door. She turned to him one last time. "I'll miss you."

"I'll miss you too." He ran his finger across her lips. "I will call you soon, sweetheart. This isn't goodbye."

How could he read her? How did he know it was what she most needed to hear?

"Sweet dreams," he said.

"You too. Good night."

"Night." He turned and went down the hall.

She closed the door and leaned against it. The cabin was quiet and empty.

Kara packed her suitcase and set it outside the door for the cabin steward. The bags had to clear customs before they could re-enter the United States. She laid out winter clothes for tomorrow and packed her carry on.

Viv came in as Kara zipped it.

"So," Viv plopped on her bed, "Are you ready to go back to the real world?"

"No. Not really."

*It was like waking up from a dream to face the real*

*world.* Her shrunken world where nothing ever changed. But she'd grown and no longer fit into that world. She had to go back to her job and her boss. God help her. She dreaded seeing Daryl.

If only the captain could sail her away, anywhere far away from Ohio. For the first time in her life, she didn't want to go home. But she had no other choice.

They went to bed and set an early wakeup call to be sure to have breakfast before they disembarked. Kara slept though restlessly and dreamed about her job going wrong.

As they disembarked, Kara suddenly sensed Nate wasn't far behind her. Even in a crowd his presence was compelling. She turned as she heard his laugh, and her gaze flew to where he stood, their eyes meeting across the crowd.

He waved and she waved back. She wanted to go to him, but the crowd wedged them in like sardines, and the large family behind her kept pushing.

"Come on, Kara, we have to keep moving," Viv said.

Kara sent Nate a look of regret.

"You're pining like a love sick puppy," Viv said. "It's over, let it go."

"It's not over. He's going to call me," Kara said.

"They all say that. If I had a dollar for every time

I heard that one, I could take us both on another cruise."

"Well, that would be nice, seeing as I took you on this one."

Here was the opening for a thank you. As Kara waited for it, with no response from Viv, it became clear that a thank you was not going to come.

*Good thing you don't have those dollars because I wouldn't want to go on another cruise with you. Once is enough. Right now I just want distance.*

They made their way down the exit ramps and into the room that held luggage. It didn't take long to find theirs.

Kara looked about for Nate but he'd already gone. How long would it be until she saw him again? *Maybe Viv was right.* Maybe he would forget all about her.

*But one thing was certain.* She'd never forget him.

# CHAPTER SIXTEEN

*K*ara waited at Viv's apartment for the taxi driver who was now fifteen minutes late. Her cell phone rang.

*Oh, good. It's the cab company.*

"Hello."

"Ma'am could you give us your address again? And the nearest cross street?"

Kara rattled off the number again.

"He'll be there in eight minutes."

"Thank you."

She waited and another text came through her phone from Nate. *Wish you could stay a few more days.*

She texted back, *I do too.*

*Then stay.*

*I can't, I have to go back to work.*

His third text came in just as she sent hers. *Don't go.*

*Where was the damn taxi?*

Maybe the fact it wasn't here was a sign she wasn't supposed to go. She certainly couldn't stay at Viv's apartment another night. One night had been enough, both of them tense and stepping around each other. They'd had pizza and watched a movie, which still hadn't been relaxing. Viv was ready for her to go and she was more than ready. They'd gone to sleep and Viv had headed off to work early in the morning after a quick goodbye.

The taxi service called again.

"Hello, is there a problem?"

"No problem, ma'am. He's just having trouble finding your apartment. Are you out front?"

"Yes, I've been out front for 45 minutes now, waiting, and I have a 12:30 flight."

"We'll have you there in plenty of time."

*And if I miss my plane I'll know I'm supposed to stay.*

Nate's words rang through her head again. *Stay. Just a few more days. Don't go.*

*Maybe I shouldn't go. Not yet.*

The taxi driver pulled up in front of her and she pushed the thought away as he got out to load her bags. She'd make her flight. It was a 45-minute drive to the airport, but she'd make it. This was just one of those days when things went a bit bumpier than usual.

Inside the cab she leaned back against the seat after giving the driver her airline and flight time. Palm trees flashed by, blue sky and clouds and then they were on the highway, leaving it all behind, the driver losing no time as he cut across lanes and sped up.

They reached the airport, but he was going too fast and drove past the drop off point where she should've gotten out to check the bags with her airline. "Hey, my flight is North point, remember?"

"Sorry miss. It's, it's back the other way now. I cannot back up."

*The street was one way. Of course he couldn't.*

"Well, you can circle back around."

"No, miss. I cannot."

*Damn it.*

This was making her later still and now she had to schlep her bags all the way to the other end.

*Well, there goes your tip, buddy. Thanks a lot.*

Kara paid him, collected her bags, and started walking. The hot, Florida sun beat down, and the jeans and top she'd worn because she'd be going back to a colder climate clung to her body as she pulled her carry on and the bag she would check, their wheels rolling along behind her.

She reached the counter and caught her breath. It was okay now; she was going to make the flight. All she had to do was check her bag and get inside where the A/C was, get something cold to drink, and everything would be fine.

"Your bag is over the limit by five pounds. It's a ninety dollar charge."

*Oh, no.* Her credit card was maxed. She couldn't pay it.

"I'll have to take some things out then."

"Maybe you can fit them into your carry on."

She opened her bag and started pulling things out. Books, souvenirs, seashells, and the edible panties.

*Oh God. That needed to go into the trash.*

She tossed them in the trash container.

"You're throwing that away?" The attendant rescued the edible panties. "My wife would like these."

"Keep them. I'm glad to be rid of them."

Maybe that's why she was having difficulties. Those things were bringing her bad luck. Once she was rid of them, everything would go smoothly again.

Now that the other bag could be checked, she busied herself with stuffing all she could into her carry on. The seams bulged.

*Hope it doesn't break.*

The attendant held out her ticket and ID. "You're all set. Gate seven."

"Thanks." She took the ticket and ID and stuffed them into the pocket of her jeans. The cool air of the airport felt good as she stepped inside and moved over to the line for security.

*What I'd give for a nice cool drink right now.* But there was no point getting anything to drink before she went through security, because they'd just take it away the moment she got there. Everything seemed to go smoothly as she went through and she waited on the other side for her bag.

*What's taking so long?*

A female security officer went over to her bag. "Is this your bag?"

"Yes."

*What now?*

"Please follow me."

*If things keep happening I'm never going to make my flight. Random searching happens. Of course it had to happen to me right now.*

The officer opened the bag and pulled out three paperback books. "These won't scan."

*Yep, got to worry about those folks who travel with books. You just never know about them.*

"Well, they're just books."

"We still have to check." The officer ran the wand around, pulled more things out, until finally she was satisfied. "Hope you can get everything back in there."

"Me too." *No thanks to you.*

Kara stuffed the bag again, jamming things in

until it closed, then hurried for the tram to take her to the terminal where gate seven was.

On the tram she exhaled and leaned against the wall. *Oh, for a good cold drink.* Once she reached her gate, she'd get a drink and something to eat. She hadn't eaten all day and it was lunchtime.

She exited the tram and hurried to gate seven, which was of course at the end of the terminal. The closer she got, the more a sense something was wrong grew.

It was the last gate in the terminal.

It was also the wrong airline, the wrong flight number and the wrong destination.

*Oh shit.*

Kara reached into her jeans pocket and pulled out the crumpled ticket.

*Gate seventy-four. Oh shit.*

Panic hit her. She was going to miss her flight.

*Seventy-four was nowhere near seven.*

She started to run back to the tram.

The tram only went one way. She turned to a security guard.

"I took a wrong turn. How do I get to gate seventy four?"

He pointed. "You have to go back through security."

She took off running again.

*Oh shit. I'm not going to make my flight.*

Waiting in line at security, the thought came

again. *Maybe I'm not supposed to make this flight. Maybe I'm not supposed to be on that plane.*

Again Nate's words rang through her mind.

*Stay. Just a few more days. Don't go.*

Then it was her turn to go through security again and her attention went to making it through. Once she through, she ran to the tram, which would take her to gate seventy-four. She reached it just as the doors closed and it pulled away.

*Oh God. Just missed it.*

Thirsty, hungry, sweaty, tired, she closed her eyes.

She felt as if she was in some movie that kept rolling, and she'd never get to the end or the credits.

*What if it was a mistake to go?*

She sent Nate a text. *Having trouble. Might not make my flight.*

He texted her right back. *You could stay with me. I would come get you.*

The next tram rolled in and the doors opened. She stepped inside. The doors closed.

*Is this all our lives are? Step on the tram, step off the tram, move to the next spot, just keep moving? Why is there never time to sit still and think?* How could she think what to do when running?

*There's no time.*

The tram stopped and the doors opened. Out the door, she took off at a run, passing all the places where she could get a drink. At this point she'd be lucky to reach the gate and make her flight.

Her clothes clung to her as she ran, the carryon bumping along behind her as she wove in and out of the crowds moving both ways.

And then she reached it. Gate seventy-four. Right airline, right flight number, destination and time.

*Ten minutes to be on board.* She ran into the ladies room, hurrying as fast as she could to take care of things, then hurried out again.

*Five minutes.* She spotted a small stand with drinks and sandwiches at the end of the terminal.

*No line. Maybe because no one wanted to eat that food.* But her stomach growled and her tongue felt like sand paper it was so dry.

Kara bought a cola and a chicken salad sandwich and hurried to board, just in time.

She found her seat on the isle, the two seats next to her, empty. She heaved her carryon into the overhead bin and then sat.

*Whew. Made it. On the plane.*

*A text came through from Nate.* Did you make your flight?

She texted back. *Yes.*

She opened her cola and drank from it thirstily then opened her sandwich and took a few bites. Nothing to get excited about, but flying on an empty stomach wasn't a good idea. She got nervous enough.

The people who had seats next to her approached and she put the cap on her cola, thrust it into the bag and stood to let them in while she waited for them to stow their bags.

*How silly.* Of course she had to go home to her job, her bills, her house.

Even if she did want to start over somewhere else. *Even if there was Nate and Florida seemed a nice place to live.*

She had to go back to work and sell her house. She was doing the right thing. The sensible thing. *Anyway, Nate had a life of his own.*

They were seated and she sat again. The moment she sat, reaching for her seatbelt, the bag fell sideways and cola spilled all over her jeans and the new white sweater she'd bought to throw on if she got chilly.

*Oh shit. Cap must've been loose.*

She'd probably ruined the new sweater. *There was no way to change now or to wash the sticky stuff off.* As if she wasn't sticky enough after running through the airport, now she was sticky from cola and had a soggy sandwich. It was as if some invisible force had dumped the cola on her the minute she started thinking she belonged in Ohio. She looked down at her hands, wondering if this could be a message. A feeling crept in. A feeling she'd made a mistake.

The woman next to her handed her a napkin from her purse and Kara thanked her. As she wiped off what she could, one last text came through her phone before she had to shut it off.

*Be safe.*

She held the phone, thinking again what a wonderful man he was. Maybe she'd made a mistake. Maybe she really wasn't supposed to be on this plane.

She closed her eyes and sat back, suddenly exhausted. Completely exhausted and strangely sleepy.

For the first time in her life, she dozed off on a plane as it took off. Fear didn't enter her mind once.

It was the bumpiness that woke her. The man next to her commented the plane needed to get up higher to get out of this weather.

*What's going on?*

She frowned and looked out the window just as the plane hit another air pocket. The two men seated on the isle seats in front of her were talking about the rough ride, showing concern.

*What if this plane is meant to crash and I'm not supposed to be on it? What if I never see Nate again? How fast we can be taken away. What am I doing here?*

Her stomach clenched. She closed her eyes and sent up prayers for safety and protection.

They hit another bump and her stomach did a flip.

*It's okay; it's going to be okay. It's like Nate says. Why be afraid of something that might happen? Fear is for things that are happening. Everything else is just you scaring yourself.*

Every time they hit another bump she repeated the words in her head.

*It's just a bump. Everything is fine.*

After a while, the bumps smoothed out and the attendants were able to start beverage service. Kara got up to use the restroom.

It felt so good to wash her hands, dab wet paper towels on her sticky jeans, and run some water onto her sweater with the hope it wouldn't stain.

Back in her seat she asked for water and took the peanuts offered. The sandwich was a lost cause so she gave the whole bag to the attendant to throw away, cola and all.

She flipped through a magazine, listening to the passengers next to her as they murmured to each other. She wasn't trying to listen, but they were so sweet to one another and in love.

An ache far greater than her rumbling stomach settled within her. One longing to be filled.

Why was she leaving when he could be the one, the love of her life, the one she hungered for?

AT LAST THE PLANE LANDED. She checked her phone again. Daryl had left texts and phone messages. She dreaded talking to him. He wanted to pick her up at the airport.

She texted back. *No. My car is here.*

Kara looked out the window at the black, barren trees and the ground covered with snow. Ohio in January was a cold, unwelcoming scene. Gray sky and skeletal trees. They'd already received two inches of snow while she was gone and more was coming down.

*Wish I'd paid extra to park in the parking garage instead of this lot.*

She reached her car, found her car keys, opened the trunk, and retrieved the scraper then cleaned off the snow on the windows and doors. It wasn't until she was done that she noticed the two flat tires.

*Oh no. Both tires flat. Of all the bad luck.* She called it in to her road service.

"Ma'am we have you on the list, but it's going to be at least four hours. Can you find a warm place inside to wait?"

"I can't wait here four hours. I have to get home."

"Sorry."

She hung up and called for a taxi. Even if she had the car towed tonight none of the tire places would be open.

*This homecoming was already not going well.* She wished more than ever she'd stayed in Florida with Nate.

KARA WANDERED into her kitchen and checked the fridge. *One can of strawberry diet shake and a diet cola.* A liquid diet was not what she had in mind tonight. Opening cabinet doors and the freezer to look in, she sighed.

*There's nothing to eat in this house.* Once her car was fixed she'd have to go to the grocery store.

She ordered a pizza and tried to call Viv, but the line was busy. She left a message saying she'd made it home okay.

Kara showered, put on warm flannel pajamas and her robe, and turned on the TV while waiting for her pizza. Her phone rang.

"Hello?"

Nate's voice rumbled through the phone line, "Hey, yellow bird."

"Hey, Nate." She smiled and leaned back against the brown tweed sofa.

"I wanted to be sure you arrived home safely."

"I'm trying to stay warm in this winter chill, but I'm fine. It's good to hear from you."

"Is your heat on?"

"Oh, yes." Her body warmed as his voice moved over her like an electric blanket. *It is now.*

"There's no snow down here. Going to be sunny and seventy. I heard you're going to get hit pretty hard."

She could listen to his voice all night. "Oh that's not good."

"Why, what's wrong?"

"I had to take a taxi home because no one can fix a flat tonight, so my car is still at the airport."

"Damn. I wish I'd been there."

"I do too. It's been a long evening. I wish I didn't have to go in to work tomorrow."

"Then call in sick. Take one more day for yourself."

"No, I really can't. The work will have piled up. I have to go in."

Nate kept silent for a moment before speaking. "You worried about Daryl?"

"A little."

"Do you want to talk about it?"

A knock sounded on the door. "My pizza is here."

"I'll wait while you get it."

She put the phone down and went to answer the door, paid for the pizza, and closed the door again. The pizza smelled so good. She picked up the phone. "Okay, I'm back."

"What kind of pizza did you get?"

"Pepperoni. My favorite."

"Sounds delicious. Well sweetheart, I'll let you go so you can eat, but I want you to know you can call or text me any time of night or day. I always have my phone on."

"Thank you."

"Are you all locked in for the night?"

"Yes."

"Good. Will you call me tomorrow and let me know how you are?"

"Yes, I will."

"And if Daryl gives you any problems, you call me, okay?"

"Okay."

"Good night, yellow bird. Enjoy your pizza."

"I will. Good night, Nate." She hung up and opened the pizza box, reaching for a slice.

*He'd called. Viv was wrong. Nate hadn't been giving her a line. It wasn't over.*

She turned on the weather channel proving Nate right. The weatherman predicted a huge snowstorm. Maybe she'd get snowed in and wouldn't have to face Daryl for a few days. She could clean the house and get it ready to put on the market. *A snowstorm wasn't always a bad thing.*

Her phone rang. "Hello?"

"Did I wake you? Are you in bed?" Daryl said.

Kara muted the TV. "No, I was catching the weather, but I'm tired and won't be up long."

"You should know we're expecting a snowstorm. You need to leave early tomorrow before the road gets bad."

"Right." Kara glanced at the clock. *Eleven fifteen.* She hoped he wouldn't talk too long.

"Do you have snow tires?"

"No, but it wouldn't matter if I did."

"Why is that?"

Uh. She'd slipped. *Great.* She was too tired to fabricate and unaccustomed to making things up anyway.

"Because my car has flats."

"You'll need a ride to work. I'll pick you up."

"No, Daryl." She stood, clicked off the TV and paced across the room. "I'll take a taxi."

"Don't be ridiculous. I can give you a ride. Be ready at seven thirty."

How could she tell her boss she didn't want to ride with him? "Well, all right."

"Get some sleep. I'll see you in the morning."

"Good night." As Kara hung up the phone, her shoulders sagged. If Daryl wasn't her boss, she'd have said no. But she needed her job, so how was she supposed to do that?

*It took time to find a new job and it was easier to find one when you already had one.*

But she needed to find one. Soon.

# CHAPTER SEVENTEEN

*K*ara couldn't sleep. She paced in the living room, then stopped, stood still and glanced around at the furniture. The masculine brown and tan stripes showed Neil's tastes, not hers. She didn't want to live here anymore. *Nothing about living here felt right.*

She went to the kitchen, picked up a pad and pencil, and started a list of things she could sell. A list of actions for tomorrow.

*First, list the house with a realtor.*

*Second, create a resume.*

*Third, list furniture to sell. Most of the furniture could go.*

She'd start somewhere new, leave her old life behind, and take only the things that made her happy.

It was time to leave her past in the past. The house, which had once given her a sense of security, now felt restrictive.

Could she stand staying at the job long enough to sell the house? *And what then?* Though Daryl now made her nervous and she'd rather not spend another moment with him, she still needed a good letter of recommendation. She hadn't worked any place else since she graduated from high school.

She realized she'd been pacing again. Well, she wouldn't get any sleep this wound up. She went into her bedroom and fired up her computer.

*Might as well get started.*

She began listing furniture she wanted to sell. When Kara finally climbed into bed and set her alarm, it was two a.m. She snuggled down under the covers up to her chin and thought about calling Nate, but it was late to call. Then exhaustion took over and she fell asleep.

THE ALARM WENT OFF TOO SOON.

The beginning strains of a headache pulsed behind her eyes as she got out of bed to turn off the alarm. She'd slept restlessly, having strange dreams.

Tired eyes gazed back at her from her bathroom mirror. *This is going to be a long day.* She missed the warm rays of the Caribbean sun.

The phone rang. *What now?* "Hello?"

"Did you just get up? You don't sound awake. I'll be there in fifteen minutes." *That's right.* Daryl was giving her a ride to work.

"I'll be ready."

She hung up and rummaged through her closet in a hurry. None of her clothes suited her. She missed the colorful styles of the Caribbean. It was hard to come back to the cold, bare lines of the trees covering the landscape in frozen Ohio. The newscaster last night said an ice storm was probable.

Kara glanced out the bedroom window at the crusty, sparkling snow. She'd move somewhere warm, like Florida. Sighing, she pulled on a slip, hose, and a dark gray skirt, the warmest one she owned. A white blouse and gray sweater completed the outfit.

She looked into the mirror. In her tan and braided hair she didn't look as if she belonged in her old things.

She put on the new yellow banana earrings and yellow scarf. Maybe they were silly but she liked them, and they added color against the gray.

She hurried into the bathroom and washed her face.

A knock came on her front door. *Daryl is here.*

She spit the toothpaste out, anxiety coursing through her as water dripped down her chin.

"Just a minute," Kara called.

She went and opened the door and stood looking at him.

"Kara? I brought you an all grain muffin for breakfast. Since you haven't been to the grocery."

"How did you know I hadn't been?"

He stood close enough she saw a slight tic in the corner of his left eye.

"I, I guessed."

"You didn't need to bring me breakfast. Really, you shouldn't have."

"Oh, but I wanted to. I know how you like muffins. And we can't have you skipping breakfast."

"Well, thank you."

"Looks like you didn't get much sleep."

"Let's go," she said as she grabbed her coat and shrugged it on.

They walked to the car then she stood shivering under the falling snow as he unlocked and opened the passenger door. Once inside, she noticed a greeting card and a red rose on the dash.

*Oh no.*

They could never work together as if nothing had changed because it had. She regretted accepting the ride.

Daryl climbed into the driver's seat. "I missed you, Kara. I'm glad you're back."

"Daryl, please start the car, I'm getting cold."

"After you open the card." He kept his voice

shaded in neutral tones and his face closed, his expression guarded.

She put on her poker face and opened the envelope then pulled out the card. A couple stood hand in hand on a beach with a red sunset and the sea. She read the front silently. *We'll always have each other.*

She opened the card up and read the inside. *I will always be there for you. Daryl.*

*This was awkward.*

Kara forced a strained smile. His steady, watchful eyes made her nervous.

"Thank you," she said, hoping her voice wasn't shaking. "You're a good friend, Daryl." She emphasized the word friend.

"Now I'll start the car." He patted her knee, and she froze. "I know you're cold."

Kara listened as Daryl caught her up to date on things she'd missed at work. Things she no longer cared about. She forced herself to depict an interest and an ease she no longer felt. *He went on and on.* How had she ever found him interesting?

She nibbled on her muffin and stared out the window as her head, which had started a steady drumbeat, showed signs of growing worse.

"We'll go to dinner after work and then to the grocery."

*What? Have I missed something?*

She glanced at his assured profile. "Daryl, I don't..."

He cut her off. "Don't tell me it's too soon to date." His expression darkened with an unreadable emotion. "I saw you with Nate." He almost spit the name. "I know you're dating. You've never given me a fair shot." He shook his head. "Not once."

*He's twisting things. This was always a work relationship, nothing more.*

"You haven't been playing fair." His eyes met hers, and then he smiled. "You can't say no this time. There's no excursion and I've already made the reservations."

The pounding in Kara's head felt as if elephants were running across it.

*I can't handle this. I just want to go home and call in sick to work for the next five hundred years. I'd like to tell him I wouldn't have dinner with him if he were the last man on earth. But the job. I need the job.*

"Yes, fine," she muttered just so he'd be quiet.

If she could just get to the office and out of this car. She never had to get into this car again. She'd get her own way home.

Tomorrow she'd call in sick. The way her head pounded she must be coming down with something. Her stomach hurt. She looked at the half eaten muffin in her hand and wondered if she was having an allergic reaction. Whatever it was, she stopped eating.

Daryl leaned back in his seat and drove without speaking.

Kara closed her eyes. *Tomorrow I'll have to deal with this. I need to get my car, get rid of this headache, and get some sleep. Then I can cope with him.*

It was all she could do to keep the muffin down.

She stared out the front window, fingers tensed in her lap, all the way to the office. Daryl turned on the radio and heavy early morning traffic kept his attention.

At the office, Kara had only minutes to settle into her cubicle before coworkers began popping by, giving her no time to settle her thoughts. Everyone wanted to hear about her cruise.

Daryl hovered, watching her. When he didn't hover and she was alone in her cubicle, it still felt like he watched her. Then it hit her.

*He's watched me like that for years. Always watching.*

Her stomach rolled.

She wanted to scream. Taking charge of her life would take more than new clothes, colorful accessories, and a trip somewhere. She should confront him. She should report him. But he was her boss and her head pounded. She needed to lie down and get rid of this headache.

Kara took the pictures out of her purse to show everyone some of the things they'd done.

"It's good to have Kara back," Daryl said. "Even with those ridiculous looking braids."

Everyone laughed, but after he walked away to take a phone call, several of them told her she looked good.

Kara wanted to be anywhere but here. She thought back to the night she'd danced with Nate and he had sung the Yellow Bird song. She looked down at her scarf and fingered it, remembering how he'd nicknamed her. Oh, how she missed him right now.

She walked down to the break room and found aspirin. When she got back to her desk Kara called Viv. The receptionist said Viv was out of the office meeting with a client. Kara sighed with frustration then turned back to a week's worth of papers on her desk.

Very few people had come into work today. Many claimed they couldn't get out of their driveways and had taken vacation days. Daryl hovered, leaning over her cubicle

*Does he have nothing better to do than to hover like that?*

She decided to ignore him. She worked until it was nearly lunchtime. Then she flipped through the yellow pages, picked up the phone and dialed. The sooner she got the ball rolling on selling the house, the better.

"Green Pastures Realty, how can I help you?" a woman chirped in a singsong voice.

"Yes, I, I want to list my house."

"Well, dear, you've come to the right place. Let me just get some information from you."

Kara answered all the woman's questions, aware Daryl could be listening to every word. This needed to get done and she didn't want to wait. The woman would come out Saturday to look at the house and take pictures.

Kara hung up the phone, stood, and walked to the water cooler, past Daryl's office. Daryl smiled at her and she forced a smile in return.

She bent to sip from the water cooler and when she stood up, Daryl stood behind her. He waited for her to finish then smiled and bent to take a drink. He followed her back to her cubicle.

"Making calls on company time? Selling the house?"

"Yes. And I'll work through lunch today." She turned back to her desk; irritated he'd eavesdropped. He knew she didn't goof off on company time. If anything she gave the company too much.

"I'll order lunch in."

She shook her head. "No thank you. I'm not eating. I'm not hungry."

"You're cranky coming back to work after that cruise. Maybe you shouldn't have gone." His hands closed around her shoulders and she froze. "Such tension." He rubbed her shoulders.

She shrugged him off. "Daryl, that's inappropriate."

He bent down and whispered in her ear, "Everyone on this floor has gone to lunch so there's no one to see."

His words sent chills down her spine and his breath on her neck gave her goose bumps that made her skin crawl.

*Oh my God.*

"It should feel good."

"Well, it didn't."

"You've had that headache all day. Did you take anything for it?"

"Yes."

He turned her chair around and leaned one hand on each side of the chair arms. "You need to relax more, Kara."

She pressed back into the chair, wishing it could swallow her and take her away. She scowled up at him.

"All right, I'll leave you alone for now." He turned and went back to his office.

She still had to confront Daryl about the edible panties, but she didn't quite know how.

*Be brave, Kara. Remember what Nate taught you. It's never as bad as you think it will be. Tell him. Do it. Get it over with. Since no one else is here, it's as good a time as any.*

She inhaled a deep breath and walked to the door of his office. "Daryl, there's something I need to discuss with you."

"Go right ahead." He gave her his entire attention.

She swallowed then forced the words out. "On the ship, someone sent edible panties to my room anonymously."

"Huh. Imagine that."

She hesitated. "I, I thought it might have been you."

"Describe the panties. What flavor?"

"Strawberry."

He smiled, and his eyes glowed as if he could picture her in them. "Red is a good color for you."

Kara couldn't breathe. She didn't like the way this conversation had turned. Why had she brought the panties up? She should've ignored it. The way he looked at her with that intense gleam in his eyes made her stomach hurt.

"Did you send them?"

"Me?" He gestured to himself in exaggerated innocence. "That would have been, what was the word you just used? Inappropriate."

*He sent them. But he'll never admit it.*

"I'll bet it was Nate. Probably thought you'd jump into bed with him." Daryl leaned forward. "Did you?"

*It's none of his business.* Angry with him and with herself, she clenched her fists.

"So you thought I sent them." His tone almost purred. One side of his mouth curled slowly. "Did you keep them?"

"No. I gave them away." She turned and went back to her desk.

Kara sat, trying to calm down, not even going through the motions of working.

At five o'clock Daryl entered her cubicle. "I'm taking you to Antonio's."

"No. I'm not hungry." Her stomach growled, betraying her. She stood, heading for the ladies room. "Uh, excuse me."

In the ladies room she leaned on the sink and looked at herself in the mirror. *What are you doing? Just tell him no. Take a taxi home.*

She closed her eyes. She had to consider her job, but he frightened her. Her pounding headache hadn't left and probably wouldn't. In fact it had gotten worse.

She'd had her car towed to a tire place but with two tires to fix, her car still wouldn't be ready till tomorrow.

*What was the right thing to do?*

She'd worked through lunch, wanting to be left alone, but also to stay busy. She couldn't lose it at the office. She'd worked here too long to burn bridges.

*If I could just sneak out and get away from here.*

The ladies room door opened and one of the secretaries stuck her head in. "You okay? Daryl said you'd been in here a while and asked me to check on you."

*I don't believe this. Can't escape to the ladies room without him sending someone after me. Is there no way to get away from him?*

"Yes, I'm fine. Tell him I'll be a few minutes."

*This is unreal. He doesn't let up. There's no privacy. No place to hide. I have to run.*

Once the secretary left, Kara opened her purse and pulled out the picture of her and Nate on the Rhino Rider boat.

*Nate, I wish you were here right now. You'd know how to handle Daryl.*

She hated being without her own transportation and needing to depend on others. *But there was a way to fix that, like calling a taxi.*

She stepped into a stall, closed the door, and called a taxi service. They'd be here in twenty minutes. She just had to get away from Daryl and wait out front.

She couldn't do this. She couldn't behave as if nothing was wrong, go on with her job, and bide her time till she found something. She had to get out of here. Now.

Peering out the door of the bathroom with her cell phone in hand, she auto dialed Daryl's office line.

The minute he walked into his office to take the call, she slipped from the ladies' room and over into the stairwell. He hadn't seen her. Three flights down and she took them at a run. She had her purse. She left her coat behind.

~

OUTSIDE THE WINDOW, snow continued to fall heavily, coating everything like a huge blanket. The moment she sat in the taxi speeding away, her nerves settled.

In the safety of her home, everything would be fine. Well, as fine as anyone without a job could be because she could not go back in there and work with him. *There was no way.* She'd use up all her sick days and then quit.

Halfway home her cell phone rang.

*Daryl.*

She didn't answer it. He left a message, which she didn't listen to. Her phone rang and rang.

The taxi driver looked at her in the rear view mirror. "Uh, somebody you don't wanna talk to?"

"Right." She put the phone on silent.

"You in trouble, lady? You don't got a coat."

"I'll be fine once I'm home."

At home, she paid the driver and he drove away.

She unlocked the front door and then paused. *The doormat was out of place.* Not up against the house but slightly back. She lifted the mat and froze.

Her spare key. It had been there when she left on her cruise. *Now it was gone. Daryl. He must have it.* And if she hadn't thought to look, she wouldn't know.

She unlocked the door, stepped inside, and then locked it behind her.

*Why hadn't Neil installed a deadbolt? With that key, Daryl could get into the house. Any time he wanted to.*

She turned her phone back on and listened to the last message he'd left.

"What the fuck, Kara? You just leave without a word? Pick up the damn phone!"

Her heart raced. In a panic, she deleted all eight messages without listening to any more of them. Her hands shook.

She closed the mini-blinds and checked the locks on her windows. She was scared. She needed desperately to talk to Nate. She dialed but it went to voicemail.

"Nate, do you remember the yellow bird that was lost in the song? She's feeling lost and alone and frightened. She's frightened because," her voice started shaking, "Oh God, Nate, I'm really frightened because I think Daryl might do something crazy. Please call me."

Kara hung up the phone. Outside something cracked and she jumped, looking over her shoulder.

A tree branch had fallen. Her nerves were on edge. The storm outside could get worse. Ordinarily she would've taken a shower after work and cooked dinner or ordered take out, then settled in to wait out the storm safe and snug in her house with a cup of tea. She couldn't relax enough to do any of those things.

She had no alarm system and didn't know how to shoot a gun even if she had one. She'd thought of getting a dog and taking self-defense lessons but hadn't gotten around to either.

Every sound made her jump. She had to do something to calm her nerves. *Tea. That was it.* She'd make tea. *A cup of tea would be good after running around outside without a winter coat.* The cold chilled her through and through. The tea would warm her up and then she'd sit down and figure out what to do next.

She laid her phone on the counter, started the water, and pulled out a tea bag and her coffee cup.

Soon the teapot whistled and she turned to reach for it, knocking her cell phone onto the floor where the glass on the front cracked.

*Oh no. My phone.*

She picked it up. *Dead.* She tried turning it back on with no luck. Nate couldn't call her back even if he got the message.

She collapsed onto the kitchen floor and sobbed.

There was no other phone in the house. The cell phone was her lifeline.

She'd never felt so alone in her life.

Alone and terrified and with no way to call the police if she needed help or to call anyone else, even a taxi to take her away.

She lost track of how long she cried.

*It wasn't safe to stay here.* She had to get away, where there were people. She stood and wiped the tears from her face.

The news forecasters predicted it would get much worse outside before it got better.

*It was going to get worse before it got better. I have to get out of here and away from any place he can find me before it gets worse.*

She prepared to run.

KARA WAS COLD AND FRIGHTENED. She'd knocked on her next-door neighbor's door planning to ask to use the phone before she realized all her phone numbers where in her broken cell phone. She didn't have an address book. *Did anybody have those anymore?* How could she call anyone she knew?

She needed a computer and not the PC sitting on her desk in the house. Even if she'd had a laptop she could take with her, she still needed Internet connection.

*The library.* She could get online there, find Viv then through Adam find Nate. *He'd know what to do.* She had to get away from her house before Daryl came. She knew he'd come to her house tonight and he was so angry.

Wrapping her scarf firmer around her head, she passed through the neighbor's back yard and headed for the alley that would lead to the small shopping area with a Laundromat, a Chinese place, and a used bookstore. The bus stop was one block down, and if she hurried she might catch the bus.

NATE NOTICED the light on his cell phone go off as it vibrated on the bar where he'd left it. He'd forgotten it when he went out for a ride. The fact he'd been missing Kara already and he hadn't been on land with a chance to ride his bike had sent him out for fresh air. He liked riding, getting away from everything and often forgot his phone.

He picked the phone up and smiled when he saw who had called.

Kara.

Her voice came through as he played back his message and he lost the smile. *His woman sounded terrified and she was hundreds of miles away.*

He called back but got no answer. Again no answer. A third time, but he wasn't getting through to her. He called Adam's cell next, thinking Adam would have Viv's number and Viv might know what was going on in Ohio. Adam's phone was turned off.

*Damn it.*

Nate dialed his friend, Johnny who ran a small airport in Florida. His assistant, Melba, picked up.

"Melba, you're working late."

"Where else would I be?"

"Melba, I'd love to shoot the breeze with you any day but today I need a favor. I have to get to Ohio tonight. It's an emergency."

"What kind of emergency?"

"The woman I love is in danger."

"I'll find Johnny and call you right back."

"Thanks."

Suddenly he realized what he'd just said. *The truth of it sank in deeper.*

He loved her. He loved every nervous little bone in Kara's body. He loved everything about her.

Nate grabbed his duffle and stuffed a couple things into it. He'd be out the door in less than five minutes. Hell, he'd traveled with nothing more than a toothbrush before.

His phone rang. *Melba.* "What have you got?"

"Commercial flights are grounded into Columbus, Dayton, and Cincinnati."

"I figured that." Nate grabbed his jacket and duffle and headed out the door. "Get me whatever you can."

"I'll see how close we can get you."

"Thanks, Melba. I owe you."

He jogged the flight of stairs down to the parking garage, swung a leg over his Harley, inserted the key, fired it up, and headed for the airfield.

In Ohio he'd find a rental car. He and the Harley raced off into the wind.

A small plane was ready and waiting when he arrived and then they were off. Halfway there ice formed on the wings and the little plane fought through the weather.

Nate worried about what might be happening at Kara's house.

If Daryl did anything to hurt her, Nate would kill the son of a bitch. His stomach twisted at the thought of anything happening to her. She was no match for Daryl and he doubted she knew how to defend herself.

In the darkness below he saw tiny lights, which indicated the landing field below. They were just about to land at a private airfield in Kentucky, across the river from Cincinnati, which was as close as the plane could get in this weather. He reached around behind his seat to grab his duffle and sat it on his lap as he waited with impatience.

The plane had barely pulled to a stop, when he pushed the door and jumped out. Nate yelled over his shoulder to Johnny. "Thanks, man."

"No problem."

Nate sprinted toward the small terminal on the edge of the narrow runway. From this point on he had to travel by car or truck.

Melba had come through for him once again. A truck with four-wheel drive waited in the parking lot, gassed up with keys on the seat.

When he got back, he'd treat Melba to a night at the horse races she loved so much. Hell, he'd give her all his money to bet on the ponies if he could only reach Kara before something happened.

Thoughts of what could happen to her filled his imagination and fueled his worry as he fired up the truck and spun out of the parking lot into the swirling snow.

NATE PULLED into the driveway of Kara's house, parked the truck, got out, and slammed the door. He raced up to the front door and pounded on it. "Kara?"

After several minutes of pounding and yelling an old woman shouted from across the street. "She ain't there."

Nate hurried across the street, but the woman stepped inside her house and slammed the door before he reached her.

"Go away or I'll call the police."

"I'm looking for my girlfriend, Kara. Have you seen her?" He shouted through the door then ran a hand through his hair in frustration, knowing he must look like hell. He'd driven straight through, three hours, only stopping once for coffee and gas. He hadn't shaved or showered since yesterday.

"I ain't saying. Now, get on out of here."

"Damn it," he muttered.

"I'm dialing 911 right now."

"You go right ahead. I'd like to talk to them myself."

"They'll be on the line any minute."

"Yes, ma'am. Please listen to me. I need to find Kara. I think she's in danger."

"You leave that pretty young thing alone. She's had enough troubles."

He paced within the confines of the tiny porch. "I know she has. I'm trying to help her."

"She don't need your help. Got herself a nice, new man, dresses nice, has a nice car too. He's a true gentleman. Brings my trashcan down to the curb for me. Always uses her back door so people don't talk. She don't need the likes of you. Come around here pounding on doors."

"I apologize. But this is important. You say this guy has been sneaking around the back of her house? Kara is my girlfriend and that guy has not been visiting her. That guy is her boss, not her boyfriend. She's afraid of him. So you go ahead and call the police, ma'am. I'd like to talk to them myself.

But in the meantime I need to find Kara and make sure she's all right."

"I don't believe a word of it. Mr. Swinford has always been so nice."

*Swinford. So that's the guy's last name.*

If he couldn't find Kara, he was going after Swinford.

He stuck a card in the woman's door. "Here's my name and number. Call me if you see or hear from her. It's important."

*She probably wouldn't. But maybe she'd have a change of heart if she thought it over.*

*So the son of a bitch has been sneaking around and there's even a witness. Too bad Kara hadn't called the police. Swinford, you're not as smart as you think you are. You're going down.*

The roads were still slick and the truck skidded as he drove away, heading for Kara's office next. He slowed down. Nate found the office building then pulled into a parking garage one block over.

*If Kara was at work she'd be safe in the building with security and cameras everywhere. Daryl would avoid doing anything in front of the cameras.*

THE 24-HOUR COFFEE shop was a dive, but she didn't know where else to go. If she used her bankcards, Daryl could track her. *He knew his way around the*

*computers at the bank.* She didn't trust any of the plastic cards she carried.

There was no point in her trying to find a place to sleep, since she'd never be able to sleep tonight. The library had closed and she had to leave, but not before she sent emails to Viv and to Nate. Too bad she had no way of seeing if they'd responded yet. *Daryl had sent her messages too.* She'd deleted the rest of them without reading after she'd opened one.

*It said, Kara, why aren't you safe at home where you belong? It's not wise to be out on a night like tonight in this storm.*

*But don't worry.*

*I will find you.*

Reading his message had made her feel like throwing up. She'd had to sign off and run to the ladies room where she squatted, wrapping her arms around herself and rocking back and forth.

*Oh God, oh God, oh God. Please help me.*

Fear filled her mind and her body. He was crazy and he'd keep coming after her. He was tenacious that way and he'd decided he wanted her. *He was good at getting what he wanted.* From promotions to getting his coworkers to do what he wanted, she'd seen his aggressive side at work for years now. Having that turned on her wasn't something she wanted to contemplate.

She couldn't go back to the bank. Ever. Not even

to get her things. *Not while Daryl worked there.* She couldn't face him again.

She couldn't stay in her house. She couldn't go back there. *Not alone.*

What would Daryl do if he found her?

She tried not to think about that, but it pressed in on her, the imagined things he might do. The unknown, which was even worse because it took no form or shape in the imagination.

She knew this was the source of her fears. Imagining the worst. Ships sinking, drowning, always the worst happening, and all the thoughts that kept her hidden in a routine of work and home. A world of routine she'd thought would keep her safe from the horrors of the unexpected. Yet even here, it found her. Who'd guess a man she worked for and ate lunch with would turn into a threat?

*You have to face your fears or they'll paralyze you. Nate is right. And he knew something about facing fear.*

Her mind still raced around too much to think clearly enough to formulate a plan and the lack of sleep wasn't helping either. She knew she had to stop being afraid and do something besides hide like a frightened rabbit.

She would give anything to hear Nate's voice right now. To be in his arms again, feeling safe and loved.

*The cell phone store. I'll go and get a new phone as*

soon as it opens and then I'm going to call Nate. He'll know what to do next.

She asked the waitress for waffles and a big glass of orange juice. *Breakfast then a new phone and maybe another call to the realtor. There was no reason the woman couldn't come out tomorrow and get that listing started sooner.*

*How quickly can I get out of town? There's nothing but the house keeping me here if I don't have the job any longer.*

She'd never sold a home before. *Neil had handled the purchase of the house. Neil handled everything. Viv was right. He'd treated her like a child. He'd picked out the house as well as the furniture. He'd even picked out her car.*

Maybe she could find one of those places that bought and sold used furniture and arrange for someone to come out and buy it all. She'd pack what she wanted to keep and move to Florida to start a new life.

The waitress set her juice down.

*Even if it means I end up waiting tables, I have to get out of here. This is not my home any more.*

NATE'S PHONE rang and he answered it, cutting off the first ring.

"Kara. Where are you? Are you okay, babe?

"Yes, I'm okay." Her voice sounded tiny and tired. "It's so good to hear your voice." She was nearly crying now. "My phone broke and I couldn't--"

"Sweetheart, where are you?" He hated to cut her off, but he needed to know where she was and that she was safe.

"I'm at the cell phone store, but I can't stay here. He might find me."

"You just keep staying on the line, sweet." He swallowed as the image of her trusting eyes looking up at him while she faced her fears came back to him. He'd give anything to have her gazing at him right now, close to him where he could protect her. "Just keep talking babe, tell me where you are and where you're going. I'll find you."

"Okay, I will." Again that small sounding voice.

"You're doing great, Kara, what street are you on now? I'll put it into my GPS."

"You're in Ohio?"

"Yes. Now where are you?"

"I'm getting on the bus now. It will move too fast for GPS."

"Kara..."

"I'm going to the main library. Back to the library. It's big and full of people. It's on Grant. I, I'll stay near the front desk where the librarians are."

"Okay, babe. I'll find you." He found the library on his GPS and turned the truck around. "Just stay on the line, sweetheart."

"Yes, Nate."

"Tell me what's been happening since you got home. Everything you can think of. I'll put you on speaker phone and keep listening."

SHE WATCHED the front doors of the library and then she saw him.

*Nate.*

Her heart lurched.

He was only a few feet away moving toward the door with strong purposeful strides. She hurried out the door and then he saw her.

His eyes riveted her to the spot. Everything around her took on a clean brightness that had nothing to do with the snow. Suddenly she no longer felt the cold.

*Nate is here. Now everything will be all right.*

Kara hurried toward him and in one forward motion she fell into his arms. She wound her arms inside his jacket and around his back, searching for his warmth, his strength. Wanting to be held as she'd never been held before.

His arms closed around her, pulling her to him, holding her close, lifting her off the ground until only her toes touched before letting her back down softly.

She burrowed her nose into his neck inhaling his scent. He was so warm, so solid, and so very strong.

"Kara," he breathed into her hair. "Thank God you're safe."

*Safe. Yes, safe.* That thing she longed for that seemed always to be out of reach.

"I'm glad you're here," she mumbled and her breath bounced back off the side of his neck, along with the heat radiating from his body. She felt the movement of his breathing as her body settled into a rhythm to match his. His scent filled her senses.

Kara closed her eyes. *Safe.* She'd be safe now. As long as Nate stayed with her, but how long would that be?

*He was here now. That was what mattered.* She wouldn't think about tomorrow or if something would take him from her. *Now was all that mattered.*

Nate kissed the top of her head and caressed the side of her face with one strong warm hand. "I was so worried about you."

The soft brushing of his thumb against her cheek made Kara close her eyes. She turned her face up toward his and looked into his shining eyes, which gazed down at her with such intensity. How shiny his eyes were, as if they held tears.

"I didn't think you ever worried."

Nate blinked the moisture away and squeezed her close to his side with the arm that remained around her waist. "Come on." He pointed with his other hand. The truck is over there."

They turned and he kept his arm around her as if unwilling to let her go, even for a minute. She matched her pace to his as they crossed the parking lot.

Nate unlocked the truck and helped her inside.

As he hurried around to open his door, she wondered if he'd driven all night to get here. *He must've received her message.* He'd come all this way just for her.

Nate climbed in and started the truck. He cranked up the heat and she turned to him, tears welling in her eyes. Her chest felt as if it would burst. "I still can't believe you're here."

"Believe it, Kara. You're safe now." He riveted his concerned gaze on her face for several seconds before inspecting her from head to toe. His voice broke with huskiness. "Are you cold?"

"Not anymore."

His hand reached out to cover hers on the bench seat. He grinned that slow grin that melted her heart and made her toes want to curl.

"I'm glad you're all right." His voice wrapped around her like a warm blanket as he squeezed her hand.

Kara sighed and leaned back against the seat. There was no place in the world she'd rather be than right here next to him.

He released her hand to drive and once out of the parking lot he glanced at her again. "Are you hungry?"

Kara couldn't tear her gaze from his profile. No one ever looked better to her than Nate did right now. Her eyes drank him up and her breath caught in her lungs as it hit her. She'd lost her heart to this man. She loved him and she'd follow him anywhere. She'd fallen so hard she might never recover if anything took him from her.

His deep-timbered voice resonated in her ears, and his eyes held so much feeling.

A warm glow settled over Kara as the heat from the truck mingled with the heat his words created in her.

A part of her wanted to revel in the love she felt for him, but her feelings were too intense. *It was dangerous to love like this, so completely.* She'd loved Neil, but not with this depth of feeling. She'd never felt this out of control. Ready to pack a bag and follow a man she'd only known for a week. If losing Neil had devastated her, what would losing Nate do to her?

How did she know some crazed gunman wouldn't shoot Nate when he was doing something ordinary like pumping gas? How did she know he wouldn't die tomorrow in some horrible diving accident?

She closed her eyes and leaned into the seat,

trying to will away her fears. She wanted to be safe, happy and with Nate. She wanted a safe, normal life.

*Now he was here.* He came all the way to Ohio for her just when she needed him most. Could it mean they had a future together? Dared she hope for that?

It was her greatest wish of all that they'd be together until they grew old.

How fast she'd fallen for him. So fast it scared her. She wanted this so much.

When the truck came to a stop and Nate turned off the engine, Kara opened her eyes.

His gaze was soft. "I thought you were asleep."

"No. Just thinking."

His warm hand closed over hers as his eyes examined her as if searching for something. "Sweetheart, are you really all right?"

She nodded, wanting to cry at his endearment and the concern in his voice. *This wouldn't last. It couldn't. Nothing lasted.* Her emotions had been all over the place from the moment she reached the airport. Beneath his warm gaze they now started to settle.

"Then we'd better get you inside where it's warm." Nate slipped out of the truck and came around to open her door. She watched him through the truck windows, unable to take her eyes off of him. How many more days would they have together before he went away?

He opened her door and held out his hand as he

tipped his head, assessing her. "You have such a serious look on your face."

She put her hand in his warm palm and he helped her down with the other hand on her waist.

"Careful, there's a slick spot." He held her elbow as she stepped to the sidewalk. He pulled her around to face him and pulled her close. His eyes gazed down into hers.

She moistened her suddenly dry lips with her tongue, almost without realizing it.

He looked into her eyes for a moment then bent toward her and she knew he'd kiss her. Her breath caught and her lips parted as she waited for his kiss.

His lips brushed hers gently before he murmured, "I've missed you, Kara."

Her knees weakened.

"I couldn't stand the thought of anything happening to you."

Kara knew the feeling. She felt the exact same way about him.

Back inside her house, Nate settled beside Kara, linking his fingers through hers. His thumb rubbed circles on her palm.

Kara closed her eyes and leaned her head back against the couch. If only they could stay here like this. She was warm, relaxed, and with each circle of his thumb a tiny bit more of her came alive. She lay with her eyes closed and thought; soon he'll kiss me again. *And I'd like that, if only I wasn't so tired.*

KARA AWOKE on the couch and sat up.

Nate stood up from the recliner and rolled his neck.

"How long have I been asleep?"

"A while. But you needed it."

"Sweetheart, I'm going to pick up some equipment and then sweep over your house to look for bugs." He held out his palm. "I've already found one."

She peered at the strange object. "It's so small."

"Yep."

"Where was it?"

"Right under this lamp."

"Nate, this is really frightening." She stood. "Can I come with you?"

"I'm not leaving you here by yourself."

THE FEELING he was being followed nudged Nate.

He glanced in the rear view mirror and decided to test the driver in the small, brown car that followed each lane change and exit he took. He pulled off the highway and into a gas station despite having a half tank of gas.

"What are you doing?" Kara asked.

"Thought that car might be following us."

274

The brown car pulled into the gas station across the street.

Nate's eyes narrowed as he drove away and the brown car kept going down the street in the opposite direction.

*Too late, pal. It's easy to spot the pattern if you know what to look for.*

"Was it?"

"Nothing to worry about, sweetheart. Let's go check out your house."

Nate pulled into the drive, then he got out and opened Kara's door. He'd be on guard but would downplay this to Kara.

*She's been scared enough.*

He wasn't going to be the cause of scaring her further.

Once inside the house, Nate went over each room thoroughly, checking for bugs and cameras. Each time Nate found another piece of surveillance equipment, he cursed. Her computer was compromised and there were cameras in the kitchen and bathroom. But her bedroom was worse.

Kara stood in the doorway of the bedroom with her arms wrapped around herself, her face pale beneath her tan, her eyes wide.

Nate wanted to throw something or better yet, pound the life out of Daryl. Still the sight of her helped him control his rage toward the man.

"I can't stay here," she said. "I don't ever want to sleep here again."

He quietly said, "You won't have to."

Relief flooded her face.

"This is serious. It's time to call the police."

DARYL THREW the remote control across the room where it hit the wall, breaking before it fell to the floor. He made fists as he stared at the blank TV screens.

Nate had found every piece of expensive equipment Daryl had installed in Kara's house. Rage built as the cameras went blank one by one.

He knocked over a lamp, breaking it before he gained control again, pushing his anger back down.

Soon he'd have Kara. *She'd regret running to another man.*

He liked her scared, but she was supposed to run to him. All the time he'd invested in her, being a friend after her husband died. All wasted now, because she'd run from him and no longer trusted him.

He placed a tape in the VCR, hit play. He reached under the pillow for the pair of panties he'd stolen out of Kara's dirty laundry then brought them to his nose and inhaled sharply, filling his nostrils with her scent as he watched her naked image on the screen, and began to touch himself with his other hand.

The thought of what he'd soon do to her filled him with excitement and painful anticipation. *Soon she'd be the one feeling pain.* Then he'd do as he wanted with her. How dare she run from him? She was his.

His anger built but he found a different kind of release.

NATE KEPT watch in the rear view mirror for the car that had followed them earlier but saw no sign of it. The police had finished at Kara's house and Nate was taking her to a large hotel, one with security.

Her stomach growled.

"Sounds like we'd better get something to eat first," he said.

"Can we order room service? I just want to stay in."

"Anything you'd like."

He wanted to make her as comfortable and safe as possible after what she'd been through.

The police had found no fingerprints, so there was nothing to tie Daryl to the surveillance installed in her home, but a search warrant of his home might turn up evidence.

She hadn't helped matters by deleting all Daryl's

messages, but the officer in charge had assured her, her records could be obtained from the phone company, showing incoming calls and if they were lucky, text messages.

In the meantime, until they locked Daryl away, Nate was taking no chances with the love of his life.

She didn't know it yet, but he intended to spend the rest of his life with her, if she'd have him. He'd held her last night as she'd drifted off to sleep and all through the night. Holding her next to him like that felt so good. Better than he would even have imagined.

THEY HAD JUST VISITED a different branch of her bank and she'd closed all but one account, her checking. She'd get all her bills written today and send them out. She didn't like the fact he had access to her accounts by working at the same bank. So she was opening an account at a new bank today. One that had branches in many cities, some in Florida.

Nate had suggested the bank he did banking at. What he hadn't said was he hoped she would move to Florida with him.

These errands took most of the morning and as Nate drove her around he kept an eye out for anyone who might follow them.

He had a bad feeling again.

When Kara had called a co-worker to say she was taking a sick day today, the woman had said, "Oh, do you have the flu too? Daryl called in sick with it today."

*The man was not at work and he was not at home. Yet his car sat in the drive. The police were keeping an eye out for him, but who knew where he was right now.*

Kara watched Nate. "Is something wrong?"

"Nothing I can't handle."

Nate glanced in the rear view mirror again, and she turned around and looked behind her into the truck bed. "Did something fall out?"

"No. I'm just keeping an eye on things. So, what are you hungry for? It's time for lunch."

"Oh, I don't know. Maybe chicken and mashed potatoes and gravy."

*Comfort food. Of course. What people ordered when they were upset.* How could he lighten things up for her?

"How about something more fun. Like pizza?"

She sighed. "That sounds good. What kind of pizza do you like?"

"I like them all. But I haven't tried any Ohio pizza before." He smiled. "You can teach me about Ohio. Let's pick one up and take it back to the room."

"Okay. We could get a Cassanos pizza."

His hand closed over hers. "Sweetheart, that sounds good."

"Yes, sounds good to me too."

AFTER LUNCH and a long nap Kara asked if they could go to her house and pick up some things, since it looked like they might be staying in the hotel more than one night. She didn't want to sleep in her house even with Nate there to keep her safe.

"Of course," Nate said. "If you have bath stuff bring it along and I'll run you a hot bath, then if you'd like we can watch a movie together."

"That sounds good."

They'd enjoy a quiet evening together, just the two of them cuddled up in comfortable companionship watching a movie. She closed her eyes and leaned her head back against the seat of the truck.

"You deserve some pampering." His voice deepened. "I might even give you a back rub."

Her eyes opened. "Oh, that sounds wonderful."

"Come on."

It didn't take long for her to pack a bag with the things she wanted and to collect her mail. Soon they were headed back to the hotel.

Nate pulled into the parking garage, parked, then hefted her bag and they headed toward the hotel elevator.

The parked cars were empty, the garage silent.

A brown Ford sedan raced around the curve toward Nate, the man driving holding a gun out the open window.

Dropping the bag Nate reached out and hauled Kara behind him with one hand as he pulled a gun out of his coat with the other raised it and aimed.

Kara watched frozen in disbelief.

Shots rang out. A bullet hit the door of the car beside them. Nate's shot went through the windshield hitting the gunman in the forehead. The gunman slumped forward over the steering wheel. The car crashed into a minivan and came to a halt.

"Stay back," Nate held one hand out warning her to stay and edged forward, his gun pointed at the man who was surely dead.

Kara was glad Nate was taking no chances.

He checked to see there was no one in the back seat and then opened the car door. He reached in and took the man's pulse. Then he stood and turned to look at Kara. "He's dead. Call the police."

Pulling out her phone, she hurried over to him, "What should I say?"

"Tell them there's been an attempt on your life. Tell them exactly what happened."

In the distance they could hear a siren.

"They may already be on their way."

A cell phone on the floorboards started ringing. He reached down to pick it up.

"Daryl Swinford." The caller ID showed who was calling.

Kara gasped, took a step back and pressed her hands into her stomach.

Nate held up a finger to his lips. He pressed speakerphone and took the call without speaking.

"The money is in your account." Daryl said.

Nate remained silent.

"Hello?"

Nate coughed twice.

"Tell me the job is done."

Nate coughed again.

"Damn it, speak to me. Do you have the woman?"

Nate went into a fit of coughing then hung up. The phone rang again but he didn't answer. "Hopefully I didn't spook him. If he calls again maybe they can trace it."

Kara stared at the dead man. "I've never seen that man before."

"The police will figure this out." He tucked his gun into his belt and laid the phone on the seat as the siren sounded closer. "Let's step away from the car. They're almost here."

Her hands were shaky as she held out the phone. "Do, do I still need to call?"

His concerned brown eyes gazed down into hers as he held out his arms. "Come here, baby."

She stepped into his embrace and closed her eyes as his arms closed around her. His hand rubbed her back as he stood holding her and he didn't let go even when the police car pulled up, lights and siren going.

The siren turned off and two patrolmen stepped

out of the squad car cautiously, guns at the ready as they took in the scene.

"There was a report of gunshots." The taller man spoke.

"Yes, sir," Nate answered as he released Kara. "That man made an attempt on her life." He nodded at the dead body.

"Ma'am, are you all right?"

"I am now, thanks to Nate."

The policeman eyed Nate. "Your weapon."

Nate held his hands out and turned around placing his hands on the car to allow the policeman to step up and remove the weapon.

As the man patted him down for more weapons he said, "You seem familiar with this procedure."

"Just making it easier for you, sir. I'd appreciate you taking us both down to the station where Kara will be safer."

"You'll be there soon enough."

The other officer had called in to the station and soon police officers; yellow tape and crime scene investigators ready to do their jobs surrounded them.

Kara and Nate were transported to the station in separate cars and she did not see him again for several hours.

When at last they were both released, she ran into his arms. "Oh Nate. What a nightmare this is."

He held her close and said, "It's almost over, Kara. They'll find Daryl."

Just as they were ready to leave, another police officer approached them. "Mrs. Worth?"

She turned to look at him. "Yes."

"I'm sorry, ma'am, but I have a few questions about your husbands death."

"What?"

"We have reason to believe this man is the same man who killed your husband."

She gasped.

After all this time if they could answer the questions that had haunted her so many nights.

As they sat down at the table the officer said, "I had a hunch." He tapped his pen on the table. "The man who shot your husband also drove a brown Ford sedan and the bullets were a match. Then when we checked his cell phone records we found calls made to and from Daryl Swinford just before and after your husband was murdered. We then checked his bank records. Large deposits were made to his account at the time and again this week. We believe Swinford paid this man to kill your husband."

"It wasn't a random act of violence?" Horror filled her. "It was a lie. Everything."

"Kara? Sweetheart," Nate reached for her hand.

"We believe Nate was next."

She shivered. "Oh, Nate, he would have killed you."

Nate reached his arm around her and rubbed her shoulder. "I'm not easy to kill. You wouldn't believe the near misses I've had."

She shivered again.

"We've issued a warrant for Mr. Swinford."

Kara gave him a nervous smile. "Will you call me as soon as you catch him?"

"Yes, ma'am. But don't worry. We expect to have him in custody soon."

Nate squeezed her shoulder, pulling her to him. "They'll get him. And I'll stay with you."

"Daryl is crazy. They'd better catch him soon."

"Come, Kara. We'll go back to the hotel and stay there until he's captured."

She nodded.

Later that evening, when things had settled down, he ran the bath he'd promised her. He added her bath oil, which was lavender scented.

"Smells good." He swished the water around as she watched him then announced, "Your bath is ready, my lady. Take all the time you need. I'll be right outside. Call if you need me."

He cupped her chin and looked down into her eyes. "You're going to be all right, Kara. You're safe here with me. I'm not going anywhere."

She nodded without speaking.

"All right," he stepped back with his hand on the doorknob. "Should I leave this open or closed?"

"Closed."

When he thought she'd been in there so long she might be turning into a wrinkled prune, he rapped softly on the bathroom door. "Kara?" When she didn't answer he eased the door open.

A vision greeted his eyes. Kara lay back against the wall of the bathtub; her face flushed pink, wet hair resting on her shoulders and her rosy breasts, which glistened with bath oil. She'd fallen asleep in the tub.

"Kara," he called to her softly as he stepped into the room, picking up a towel from the corner rack, not wanting to scare her awake and conscious of his immediate response to her beauty.

She opened her eyes slowly and looked into his for one brief moment then slid down into the tub and reached to cover herself with her hands as her cheeks blazed and her lashes dropped. Watching her only made his reaction intensify.

"You fell asleep. Ready to get out now?"

"Yes."

He held out a hand to her and she stood, water streaming down her body.

THE WARM WATER and the floral scented oil had made her skin soft, warm, and slippery. Made her body long for his touch. For his eyes to gaze at her again with that look that made her feel every inch a woman.

Oh, how she wanted to be kissed and held and made love to by this wonderful man. The man she loved with all her heart.

He took the towel and dried her off. It wasn't long until they were kissing and moving toward the bed.

Lightly he fingered a loose tendril of her hair on her cheek. "You're so beautiful." His eyes searched her face, reaching into her thoughts. "You were afraid." His soothing voice probed further. "And you've been afraid for a long time. But Kara," he looked deep into her eyes, "I'm hoping you won't be afraid any more. All that talk about randomness and bad things happening. What happened to your husband wasn't random."

She inhaled sharp. It was as if he'd been reading her mind, though it wasn't possible.

"It's no shame to be afraid. It's what you do with your fear that determines the outcome. And you, sweetheart, are brave. You walked out of your bank job and now you're ready to leave everything behind. Do you realize how much courage you have?"

"Maybe I have a little bit."

"More than a little, sweetheart." His thumb

caressed her cheek and his eyes softened. "You're beautiful and brave. That's quite a combination."

A warm glow flowed through her. No man had ever spoken to her this way. *He meant every word he said.* Her confidence formed a solid rock in the core of her being where once there'd been only doubt.

She was brave. She felt it inside herself now.

Her eyes glittered up at him and he bent to kiss her. She reached up and wound her hands around the back of his neck, through his hair. She kissed him back, lingering, savoring each sensation. *He was alive.* Here in front of her, warm and strong, loving her. Joy filled her soul.

His hands caressed the planes of her back as her tension eased away, replaced by a different kind of tension. One that built slowly as his fingertips traced a gentle path over her body, followed by kisses which raised that hum within her.

They kissed and touched each other, celebrating the gift of life, the gift they brought to each other until soon they both rode on a great wave of passion. She rose to meet him and together they crested that wave until it broke, leaving them both panting in each other's arms like the edge of the sea drifting in and out across the sand once the wave had moved on.

He rolled onto his side and gathered her into his arms kissing her forehead. "I love you, sweetheart."

His cell phone rang.

Nate answered the phone. "Hello?" He listened for a moment. "Hold on, I want Kara to hear this." He turned on the speaker and handed the phone to her. "It's the police."

"Yes?" Kara said, holding her breath.

"Ms. Worth, Daryl Swinford has been picked up and he's being processed as we speak. You can rest easy now."

She breathed a sigh of relief. "Thank God."

"With the evidence we found at his house, the probability of conviction is high."

"Oh, thank God." She exhaled a great sigh of relief. "What was at his house?"

"Let's just say he's been watching you for some time, ma'am. We have enough photos and video along with the other evidence to put him away for a long time."

Thanking the officer, she hung up the phone and turned to Nate with a huge smile. "Let's celebrate."

He smiled back at her. "And just how would you like to celebrate, sweetheart'?"

She leaned in for a kiss. "Like this."

SHE'D FALLEN ASLEEP AGAIN after hours of lovemaking and she woke to Nate showering kisses all over her body.

He paused, seeing she was awake.

"Kara, I love you."

Nate's words of reassurance while snorkeling came back to her. "Take a chance Kara. I've got you."

She'd take a chance and move to be with Nate. They'd talked about it. It was amazing how much talking they'd done in between making love.

Nate would take care of her. *He already had.* He was a very capable man, but he wouldn't take care of her the way Neil had, doing everything for her, treating her like a child without expecting anything of her.

Nate expected her to do things for herself. He believed in her, believed her capable of things she'd never even dreamed of. And that belief strengthened her.

She now had a strength she'd never even realized, but Nate saw it in her all along. He'd stand by her side supporting her in everything she did.

What more could she ask for?

Again his words repeated in her head. "The only way to live life is to face your fears. If you don't they will control you."

She was aware of how fear could control a person.

"I want to share my life with you. I'll stand beside you each step of the way. But only if it's what you want."

"Oh, Nate, I love you. Yes, I want to be with you, however long our forever turns out to be. One moment of this is worth everything." She closed her eyes as tears welled up.

She dared the biggest risk of all, her heart. Then Kara was in his arms, releasing all her hesitation, her fears, her thoughts as his arms closed around her, holding her tight.

Love and life could be a great adventure with the right man by her side.

KARA SAILED the seas with Nate and painted portraits of the nighttime sea.

The secret dream that had been buried beneath her predictable, safe life spilled forth like the most precious shell washed onto the sand. Painting became a part of her life and she found, to her surprise, she was quite good at it.

And in every painting she painted, up in the right hand corner was a small but bright, wishing star.

## THE END

## AUTHORS NOTE:

Thank you for taking the time to read Aboard the Wishing Star. If you enjoyed the story, please consider telling your friends and/or posting a review. Word of mouth is an author's best friend and much appreciated.

I have included a sample chapter in the back of this book for you to enjoy. Check Out is the first book in the Bobbins Sisters trilogy and features a Marine veteran and a shy librarian.

Thank you! - Debra Parmley

## SAMPLE CHAPTER: CHECK OUT: BOOK ONE: CHAPTER ONE

*Some people stock up on milk, bread and eggs when a storm is coming, but book people stock up on books.*

Betsy checked out another library patron with a stack of books and wished she'd had more of a lunch break. She'd wanted to get her tire fixed. It was low, but the tire place hadn't been able to promise to have it ready in time for her to get back to work at the Bartlett Public Library in Tennessee.

Now, she'd have to drive home on that low tire in rain that had been falling all day and had now turned to sleet, which would then turn to ice as the temperature continued to drop.

Wondering if it was starting to get bad out there, she pushed her glasses back up on her nose, tucked her dark blonde hair behind her right ear, a nervous habit of hers, and sent a worried look to the glass doors. She caught her breath and her mouth froze into an Oh.

Stomping into the library onto the floor mat, wearing boots and a fatigue jacket, stood a tall, broad shouldered man who took her breath away. Handsome, with long dark bangs that fell onto his face, he brushed the hair back impatiently with his right hand, fully revealing an eye patch over his right eye. His good left eye, a deep brown, bored with intensity into her. He carried a stack of books under one arm.

"Are you going to check me out or what?" The cranky elderly lady who was next in line brought Betsy back to what she should have been doing.

"Yes, ma'am." She reached for the first book with a shiver.

*That man let all this cold air in, that's why I have goose bumps. Was he born in a barn? And stamping there like that with his big boots drawing attention and then giving me that look. What is that look about?*

She could still feel that look. As if he'd seared it into her soul. She shivered again and finished checking out Mrs. Geraldine E. Watson. "Be safe driving home."

The woman harrumphed. "Would have been gone by now if you hadn't been googley eyeing that man. I just hope I make it home in this sleet."

*I'm not googley eying anyone.* Betsy frowned.

Betsy did not google eye men or Her shyness

prevented her from talking to men she didn't know, unless they initiated the conversation. Though she might check them out beneath lowered lids if she knew they wouldn't see her. A handsome man was a fine sight indeed.

*This man, though, where had he gone?* She glanced over to the door and then scanned from the door to the end of the line of patrons waiting to check out.

*Oh.* She took in a breath. *There he is. Right at the end of my line.*

Tension filled her. The library closing in ten minutes announcement came over the speaker, making her jump. She'd heard it so many times before, knew it was coming and yet she jumped.

*Because of him. I'm jumpy because of him. It's a good thing he's not looking at me right now. I need to settle down and finish my job.*

Processing the patron's books, she worked, refusing to look over at him again. But the tension did not ease.

Then he was there before her, with that dark, mysterious eye patch and strong intense deep brown eye looking at her as if he had x-ray vision and could see inside of her all the way to her soul.

*They say losing one of your senses makes the others stronger. Is that why his gaze makes me feel so strange? What is he seeing? I have to say something now. He's just standing there looking at me.*

This handsome stranger would have made her

297

feel shy even without his eye patch. The patch added a mysterious, raffish quality to his look. The frown he'd sent her way when he'd entered the library still resonated with her.

Now that intense eye was focused on her with a direct intensity she was not used to. Her words came out in a stammer. "D...did you enjoy the books?" She gave him a small, shy smile.

He met it with a growl. "Hell no, I did not enjoy these books." He pointed to his eye patch. "What do you think?"

"I...I surely don't know." She turned beet red. "I'm so sorry. I didn't think." She reached out for them. "Here, I'll just take them."

He handed them to her, still keeping that intensity focused on her.

Wanting to help him, she said, "We have audio books if these are too much."

"I'm not blind," he growled.

"Oh, of course not. I didn't mean to imply—" Flustered, she turned pink and patted the stack of books, her voice coming out in a squeak. "If the type on these is too small, we have large print." Her voice squeaked high on the word print as he impaled her with his gaze.

"My eyesight is fine," he ground out the words." "Oh." Totally flustered now, she put one hand to her mouth, turning even redder and said, "I am so sorry. I was just trying to help."

He blinked once, his gaze changing as he seemed to catch himself, pulling back just a tad from whatever foul mood he was in, but not enough to appear friendly. "Don't worry about it." He shook his head and growled again. "Where are the audio books?"

Wordlessly, she stood pointing to the right in the direction of the audio books. She could have stepped out of Dickens' Christmas Carol as she stood so still and solemn like the ghost of Christmas future, afraid to speak, for when she spoke, it only seemed to make things worse.

He gave her a curt nod and took off in that direction.

Shakily, she let out a breath.

*Less than ten minutes now and everyone will go home. I hope my tire makes it.*

She carried his books to the rolling cart behind her and added them to the stack of returned books piled up.

*I'll get caught up on those tomorrow. He couldn't drop the books in the return slot while the library is open because we lock it. Why people think it's funny to put their trash in that slot I'll never know. It's like unscrewing the saltshaker. Some people don't have enough interesting things to do.*

*Did he simply want to return the books, or had he stopped at the desk because he wanted something? He looked like he wanted something. But if so, he hadn't said what. Yet, he didn't seem like a man who had trouble speaking up. Why is he looking at me like that?*

She kept checking out patrons and then with one minute to closing, there he stood before her again with two audio books in his hand. A Tom Clancy, and one of Barry Eisler's John Rain books. So, he was obviously a military man who liked action adventure stories.

*You can learn a lot about a person by noting what books they check out.*

He handed her the audio books without speaking, and she checked him out. His name was Nash. Nash Ware.

*Ware. Be wary. He might be a werewolf.*

She mentally shook herself.

*Enough of the word play. I scare myself sometimes. My mind is too often in the world of fiction. He's just a man.*

"Thanks." He gave a brief nod and headed for the door.

He was the last patron out and she locked the door behind him.

After shutting down lights and computer systems and putting the phone on the answering machine, she put on her coat, slipped out of her work shoes into her new black suede boots, grabbed her purse and headed for the back door.

June had left five minutes before in a hurry to

pick up her baby and to get them home as soon as she could to be off the roads before the ice got worse. The library was quiet, dark and securely locked.

Walking to her car, Betsy nearly slipped on the sheets of ice that had formed. Her new boots proved to be more decorative than useful. Fortunately, she righted herself with some fancy footwork. Her car stood alone beneath the light, layered in a covering of snow and ice. Taking her glove, she brushed off the window and door of the driver's side and unlocked her door. A big black Jeep was at the parking lot entrance. It backed up, and then turned around and headed her way. The Jeep had big black tires, tinted windows and was the largest Jeep she'd ever seen.

*Oh no. Who is that and what do they want? It looks like something out of the movies, like a dark government vehicle. Why are they coming toward me?*

She jumped into the car quickly and locked the door, her heart racing. Putting her key in the ignition, she cranked the engine. It wouldn't start.

*Oh, no.*

She gasped and then turned it over again. This time it started. The stereo blasted Celtic Woman, Betsy jumped and turned it off. She couldn't see through the other windows, which she hadn't cleared off yet, so she strained to see where the Jeep had gone.

A knock on her door made her jump with a shriek and flip her head around.

The man with the intense eye and eye patch stood looking down at her.

*Oh, my God. What does he want?*

He held out an ice scraper and shouted through the window. "I'm going to clear your windows."

*Oh. That's nice. I didn't expect that. But that doesn't mean I should trust him.*

"Thank you," she shouted back, not willing to roll that window down even a crack.

He moved to the front of the car and started working on clearing it. Then he moved all the way around the car, scraping the ice off and soon all the windows were cleared. She could see out again. His Jeep was large, dark and rugged looking, parked beside her in the blind spot she hadn't cleared on the windows at first.

*Just the sort of vehicle a military man or veteran would drive.*

He came back to the window and looked in. Nice as he had been, she still wasn't rolling down the window.

"Thank you," she shouted again.

He nodded and touched his hat, his dark eye watching her. He walked back to his Jeep.

She watched him go wondering why he'd still been here when she locked up. If he hadn't done such a nice thing and then walked away, she would have assigned a bad motivation to the fact he was still here when she went to get into her car. She slowly backed out of the parking space.

*Something is wrong.*

Pulling out of reverse to drive she headed for the street, but the car slid and her rear tire hit something.

His Jeep pulled up beside her. Faster than she could work out what was wrong he was out the door and knocking at her window.

"You have a flat," he shouted.

*Oh no. I should have guessed. I should've gotten it fixed at lunch, late to work or not. Now what am I going to do?*

She unlocked the door, opened it and got out of the car. As she stepped onto the icy parking lot her foot slipped.

His hand shot out and grabbed her elbow before she could fall on the ice. "Careful."

"Oh." She gasped at the contact. "Thank you." "My pleasure, ma'am."

*So, he had manners after all.*

They walked to the side of the car together with him holding her arm until they stopped and stood looking down at her flattened tire.

"It's not safe for you to drive," he said. "I'll give you a ride home."

*Wait. What?*

Flustered by all that had happened, and happened so fast, she looked up at him.

*So tall.*

Her capacity for words strung into a full sentence seemed to have left her.

*Tall and strong.*

She stared at him wide-eyed.

*And close. Very close.*

If she'd had to describe him in one word, she would have chosen intense. This man was intense.

"I...I'll just go back inside. I can call..." her voice trailed off.

Who could she call? None of her girlfriends were going to come out in this weather, and she had no family in town.

"Don't be afraid. You're safe with me." His calm, deep tone was reassuring, as well as his presence. "We haven't been introduced properly. I'm Nash. Nash Ware."

She came back to herself enough to speak. "Nice to meet you, Nash. I'm Betsy Bobbin. Thank you for your help."

"You're welcome, Betsy Bobbin." His tone was both a caress and a reassurance, which held a note of humor as a slow grin spread across his face when he spoke her name. The grin and the twinkle in his eye began to dash away the misgivings she had about accepting a ride from him. His was a kind eye, now that the intensity had eased, and the eye patch didn't make him appear as sinister without that intensity.

"Yes, that's me. One of three Bobbins sisters." He continued to grin.

"I'm the oldest." Huge snowflakes were now falling and one splattered on her nose making her blink and adding spots onto her glasses.

"Well, Betsy Bobbin." Again that grin appeared as he spoke, "Let's get you home and warm and we can deal with your car later."

She hesitated. "All I know about you is your name. That's not enough to get in a car with a stranger. What do you do, Nash Ware?"

"I'm a Marine veteran. Been back about eight months. Going to college now on the G.I. bill."

"Thank you for your service."

He nodded. "You're welcome." He spoke in a quiet tone.

She stood watching him, not sure what to do. He seemed nice enough, but still, she had only his word that he was who he said he was.

"Here." He reached into his back pocket and pulled out his wallet, flipping it open to his I.D.

She looked from him to the I.D. and nodded. "Okay. I'm just going to make a phone call first."

"Whatever makes you feel more comfortable."

She took her phone out of her coat pocket and dialed June who answered on the first ring. "Hey, June. You get home okay?"

June answered that she had.

"Good. Listen, I have a flat. And I'm still at the library. But one of our patrons, Nash Ware, was still here, and he's offered to give me a ride home."

June said he seemed like a reliable enough man, but to call her the minute she got home.

"Yes. I'll call you when I get there. Thanks, June." She hung up and then nodded at Nash. "Okay. Sorry, I just..." she shrugged.

"Do not apologize for taking precautions for your safety. Never apologize for that." He held out his hand for her again and she took it, then stepped gingerly over to the driver's side, reached in and turned the car off.

"Take anything out that might tempt a thief."
"Oh, right." She nodded with a frown. She hadn't

thought of that, but who knew when she could get back to get her car if this storm continued.

She gathered her purse, closed the driver's side door and opened the back door. Taking a bag, she stuffed the pile of books into it and went to set it on the ground beside her as her purse slid off her shoulder and down her arm.

"Here, let me take that." He reached out his hand and she handed him the bag of heavy books.

His expression showed amusement. But what did he expect? She was a librarian and loved books. Her car and her house were always full of books.

From the pile of stuff in the back seat, she

extracted another bad and began looking for her puppets. Puppy, kitten and bear all went into the bad. "Oh good, there's lion," she said, and then realized she was talking to herself.

"Lion?" he asked in that amused tone of voice.

She slipped lion on her hand and turned to face him, holding the bag. "Yes, lion. See? Grrrr."

He threw his head back and laughed which lit up his whole face. He was beautiful when he laughed. She'd never thought a man beautiful before.

*Eye patch be damned, the man was perfect.*

She gave him a huge smile in return and said, "For when I read to the children."

"Right." He nodded. "Gotcha." And that left eye gave her a slow wink.

*That is the sexiest wink I have ever seen.*

"Is that all of them?"

"All of? Oh. Yes. The puppets. Yes, it is."

*Why can't I think straight when I'm around this man? How hard is it to string a simple sentence? I probably sound like a dimwit.*

He held out his hand again.

She handed him the bag and said, "Just a few more things."

He nodded.

She turned back to the car digging for the blue dress with the white ruffled apron and the blonde curly wig that went with it all. She stood again with the items gathered into her arms.

He gave her another grin. "Halloween costume?"

"Mother Goose." Her cheeks heated. "Or Bo Peep. Depending on the occasion."

"I see."

"There's a, um, shepherds crook. In the trunk. But I can leave that."

"If you're sure now," his voice was teasing. "I'm sure."

"Okay, hand them over and I'll load them in the back of the Jeep."

She silently handed the items to him, her cheeks still warm. Strange how warm they were with how cold it was outside, and it was terribly cold. She shivered as she realized how chilled her toes now were and looked down.

*Apparently these new suede boots are not waterproof. Damn it.*

"I just need one more thing." She turned back to her car and dug through papers, a couple sweaters and a sweatshirt on the floor of the car where she found her slippers.

Her pink bunny slippers.

Turning, with her cheeks blazing, her toes freezing and snow that had now turned back into sleet falling down into her face, she stood facing him, holding the slippers.

He let out a hearty laugh. "Now why am I not surprised?"

She hung her head a little sheepishly, feeling like a twelve year old.

He took them from her and opened the passenger door on his Jeep. "Get in, it's getting worse out. I'll lock your car."

She climbed in; he placed the slippers in back and then he said, "Do you have your keys?"

"Yes." She patted her coat pocket, and they jingled.

"Good." He closed her door, locked her car and then came around to the driver's side and climbed in. Closing his door and turning up the heat, he pulled toward the street. Then he turned to her and said, "Where to?"

She gave him her address, and they chatted for a bit, then he concentrated on driving through the icy sleet that was now coming down harder.

His cell phone was sitting on the charger and it buzzed as a text came in.

"Do you mind checking that for me?" He didn't look at her as he concentrated on the road conditions.

"Sure, I'm happy to," she said. She picked up the phone and looked at it.

*Package is delayed.*

She read the text to him.

"Send back when can I expect it?"

She typed his message in and hit send.

The phone buzzed with a response. "Two more days," she read to him.

"Tell them thanks."

She typed in the message and put the phone back.

"Thank you," he said. "You're welcome."

She was wondering what "the package" was; it sounded so mysterious, and she didn't really know this guy, this Marine veteran with an eye patch. Already she was imagining a drug deal or something dangerous like in the movies. She squirmed in her seat.

*They always talked like that, using phrases like "the package."*

He glanced over at her then back to the road. "It's a replacement frame for my Harley," he said. "Oh. Okay," she said.

"I'm restoring a 2003 Harley Davidson Road King, one hundredth anniversary special."

"I don't know much about bikes. Why does it need a new frame? Was it wrecked?"

"Yes. I bought it wrecked. The frame was bent so I had to disassemble the whole bike and send the frame to Harley Davidson so they could destroy it before they'd send me another one."

"Why couldn't they just send you a new one?"
"Number of the frame has to match the number
on the engine and the title. Lots of bikes get

stolen. It's a good thing really, but it's also a pain in the ass."

"Yes, I can see that it would be." She nodded. "Were you a mechanic in the Marines?"

"No. Though I can work on some things." He shrugged.

He might not think disassembling and reassembling a motorcycle was a big deal, but she sure did.

There was something sexy and primal about a man who was capable and could fix things.

"How did the bike get wrecked?"

"No idea. I bought it before my last tour. Just never had time to work on it until a few months ago. I wasn't home much."

"I see," she said.

He drove in silence.

Betsy sat thinking of how she'd never gotten to know any Marines or guys that drove Harleys. Until now when this handsome, growly guy had walked into her library and her life with his mood. Strong, sure and more than slightly dangerous, she wondered what had made him so moody. He'd tempered himself getting control of that mood so that he was more than pleasant to be around now, but she wondered why he'd been so growly when he first spoke to her.

She was more than a little bit curious and wanted to know more about him, but he was concen- trating on the road, so she remained silent.

Though her imagination was taking her to all sorts of places. Right on the back of his bike.

NASH WARE STEPPED into the library wearing another frown and fighting another damned headache as he stomped his feet to knock the slush off his boots.

Then he saw her.

A pretty little, dark blonde with curves, wearing red-rimmed glasses which framed pretty green eyes and red lipstick upon lips formed into an oh.

Not the sort of librarian he'd expected to see behind the counter. Standing there staring at him with that pouty little oh on her face. He'd like to kiss those pouty lips.

But she was like all the other women who liked to stare at his eye patch. He was never going to get used to that. He was also probably never going to get laid again. Course there wasn't much point in trying when he kept having these damned headaches.

He'd given up on trying to finish reading any of the books he'd checked out. Reading seemed to bring them on, or maybe it was the dreams he'd been having, but whatever it was, since he wasn't enjoying reading the books, he was bringing them back to the library. He'd planned to ask if they had any of the books on his reading list, which might save him some money in the college bookstore.

The pouty little miss had turned back to the

other patrons and was checking them out and point-edly ignoring him after staring.

He got in line and waited his turn while watching her in a covert way, hoping she wouldn't notice.

*Googely eyes, huh. The old woman had to be wrong. Pouty miss didn't like that much. If I didn't have this headache I'd be tempted to kiss her.*

She was the most adorable little librarian he had ever seen.

But she was afraid of the eye patch and him. A fresh wave of pain coursed through his head.

By the time he stood before her, he was in between waves of pain. He knew he'd snapped at her and on another day he might have apologized. But he didn't. Instead, he went to the audio section with her reactions running through his mind.

*I'm not fucking blind. Damn it.*

Her reaction had angered him more than he was comfortable with. But he hated the way women looked at him now, either in fear or with pity or curiosity. And to add her to the list of women who had reacted that way, well, it was too damn much.

He'd calmed down by the time she checked him out and when he walked to his car he popped in an audio tape, thinking he'd start listening to it on the way home. If he couldn't read the fiction he enjoyed so much, he could listen on the way to appointments or to class. He'd save his eye for reading the course work and stick to that.

The story had just started to play and he would have driven off, but then he noticed that the other

librarian had pulled out of the parking lot and headed for home, and there was only one other car in the lot with his.

It had to belong to the pouty little librarian.

*I'll just wait and see that she gets her car started before I go. Where the hell is their security? She shouldn't be walking to her car at night alone, even in good weather.*

# ACKNOWLEDGMENTS

Writing is a solitary journey, for only we can write our books, but there are many who help make the creation of a book a reality. This has been a long journey as Aboard the Wishing Star was the second novel I ever wrote, and I wrote it before my first had been published, so there was much to learn and there are many people to acknowledge who helped along the way.

Thank you to Susan, Dee and Elaine from my first RWA (Romance Writers of America) critique group and all who read from the first draft to the revised story.

Thank you to Elizabeth Strout, of the Antioch Writers Workshop, for advice and critique and to the members of our writing intensive.

Thank you to the guide who took my husband and me snorkeling off the island of St. Thomas, to see the beautiful coral and fish in the restricted area. And to my husband for showing this woman with a water phobia how to snorkel.

Thank you to Charles "Tazz" Welshans for advice on Marine military tattoos and life.

Thanks to editor Ranee Clark for helping me carve and polish this manuscript. Carving six thousand words out of a manuscript is no small thing.

Thank you to my cover artist Sheri L. McGathy.

Thank you to Lucy Monroe for your friendship and mentoring.

Thank you to my family for your love and support.

And a special thank you to my readers.

I love you all.

# ABOUT THE AUTHOR

Author Debra Parmley believes "Every day we are alive is a beautiful day," and she likes to give her readers and her story people a story that ends happily.

An Air Force veteran's wife, Debra writes military romantic suspense, contemporary romance, historical romance, poetry, and memoir.

Debra married her high sweetheart, whom she asked out after a five-dollar bet. After living in five states with her husband and their two sons, and then living 23 years just outside Memphis, TN, she and her husband sold everything and now live and travel the U.S. in their 43-foot motorhome.

Debra is an adventurous writer who has sold travel and has walked the plank of a pirate ship off the coast of Grand Cayman. She has gone swimming with dolphins in Moorea, French Polynesia, has escorted a bus full of people through Scotland, and has set foot in 13 countries. She climbs lighthouses because she is afraid of heights.

You can see read about her travels on her Beau-

tiful Day Traveler blog. https://beautifuldaytraveler.
wordpress.com/

As Debra Bishop, she writes fairy tales for all
ages, fantasy, and children's books.

Visit www.debraparmley.com

# ALSO BY DEBRA PARMLEY

## MILITARY ROMANTIC SUSPENSE:

**Green Brotherhood SEAL Team XII series:**

Finding Bryce

Real Movie Hero

Saving the Bellydancer

Green Brotherhood Trilogy #1

**Brotherhood Protectors series:**

Montana Marine

Defensive Instructor

Marine Protector

Marine Protectors

Blind Trust

A Triple C Ranch Christmas Wedding

Montana Delta Rescue

Montana SEAL Protector

Montana Rodeo Protector 2025

Montana White Horse Wedding 2025

~

**Bobbins Sisters Trilogy:**

Check Out

Check In

Check Mate – 2025

~

**Single Title:**

Aboard the Wishing Star

~

**SUSPENSE -THRILLER – with Romance:**

To Catch an Elf

~

**URBAN FANTASY ROMANCE:**

Vague Directions

~

**WESTERN HISTORICAL ROMANCE:**

Gone to Texas: A Desperate Journey

Dangerous Ties

Deadly Adversaries

Desperate, Dangerous, Deadly: A Western Collection – eBook box set

Isabella, Bride of Ohio: American Mail Order Bride

∾

## 1920's ROMANCE:

**Butterflies Fly Free series:**

Trapping the Butterfly

Dancing Butterfly

Exotic Butterfly

∾

## HOLIDAY ROMANCE:

Jenna's Christmas Wish

The Twelve Stitches of Christmas – short story, fairy tale

∾

## DYSTOPIAN ROMANCE:

**The Hunger Roads Trilogy:**

Another Change of Scenery

Down a Back Road

Into the Convergence Zone 2025

~

**POETRY anthologies:**

Twilight Dips

Everything Begins in the Belly

~

**Out of Print:**

Protecting Pippa

Split Screen Scream

Protecting Zarifah

Vague Directions – short story

Tales of Deadwood - anthology

We Know the Truth, Do You? Area 51 – anthology

Wounded Heroes - anthology

Hansel & Gretel: Down the Rabbit Hole – anthology

More Monsters from Memphis – anthology

**WRITING AS DEBRA BISHOP:**

**Children's and YA:**

The Sweetest Day - Hansel and Gretel fairytale